Hogan's Goat

A Drama in Verse

by William Alfred

First produced at the American
Place Theatre in New York City

A Samuel French Acting Edition

SAMUEL FRENCH

FOUNDED 1830

New York Hollywood London Toronto

SAMUELFRENCH.COM

A. M. D. G.

for

John and Máire Sweeney

with love

Almost all of the place names in this play really exist; but none of these characters has ever lived except in my own mind. Any resemblance to any person living or dead is purely coincidental.

PERSONS IN THE PLAY

MATTHEW STANTON, *leader of the Sixth Ward of Brooklyn.*

KATHLEEN STANTON, *his wife.*

EDWARD QUINN, *Mayor of Brooklyn.*

FATHER STANISLAUS COYNE, *Pastor of St. Mary Star of the Sea.*

JAMES "PALSY" MURPHY, *Boss of the city of Brooklyn.*

JOHN "BLACK JACK" HAGGERTY, *Assistant Ward Leader.*

MARIA HAGGERTY, *his wife, the Stantons' janitor.*

JOSEPHINE FINN, *Maria Haggerty's niece.*

PETEY BOYLE, *a hanger-on of Stanton's.*

BESSIE LEGG, *a back-room girl.*

ANN MULCAHY, *Father Coyne's housekeeper.*

BOYLAN, *a policeman.*

BILL, *a hanger-on of Quinn's.*

A PRIEST, A DECKHAND, A DOCTOR, VARIOUS CONSTITUENTS.

SCENES

The action of the play takes place in Brooklyn, in 1890.

ACT I

ACT II

Hogan's Goat

ACT I

SCENE 1

*Ten o'clock, the evening of Thursday, April 28, 1890.
The parlor of Matthew Stanton's flat on the second
floor of his house on Fifth Place, Brooklyn. The set
is on two levels, the lower level containing the
kitchen of the Haggertys, which is blacked out. To
Stage Right there is a steep, narrow staircase. Enter
MATTHEW STANTON, carrying a bottle of champagne. He is a handsome, auburn-haired man in his
late thirties, dressed carefully in a four-buttoned suit
of good serge, and a soft black hat. He bounds up
the stairs and into his flat, and throws his hat on a
chair and hides the bottle of champagne behind the
sofa. The furnishings of the room are in period: the
chairs are tufted and fringed, the mantelpiece covered with a lambrequin, the window heavily draped.*

STANTON.
Katie? Katie! Where the devil are you?
Come on out in the parlor.

(*Enter* KATHLEEN STANTON, *closing the door behind her.
She is tall and slim and dressed in a black broad-
cloth suit which brings out the redness of her hair
and the whiteness of her skin.*)

KATHLEEN.
I wish you wouldn't take those stairs so fast;
They're wicked: you could catch your foot and fall—

7

I had a bit of headache and lay down.
Why, Mattie darling, what's the matter with you?
You're gray as wasps' nests.
  STANTON.

                        I'm to be the mayor!
No more that plug who runs the Court Café
And owes his ear to every deadbeat sport
With a favor in mind and ten cents for a ball,
But mayor of Brooklyn, and you the mayor's lady.
They caught Ned Quinn with his red fist in the till,
The Party of Reform, I mean, and we
"Are going to beat their game with restitution
And self-reform." Say something, can't you, Kate!

(KATHLEEN *sits down heavily, and puts her hand to her temple.*)

  KATHLEEN.
Oh, Mattie, Mattie.
  STANTON.

                Jesus! Are you crying?
I've what I wanted since I landed here
Twelve years ago, and she breaks into tears.
  KATHLEEN.
It's that I'm—
  STANTON.

          What? You're what?

  KATHLEEN.

                  Afraid.

  STANTON.

                    Kathleen,
Now please don't let's go into that again.
  KATHLEEN.
Would you have me tell you lies?
  STANTON.

               I'd have you brave.
    (KATHLEEN *rises angrily, and strides towards the bedroom.*)

Where are you going, Kate? To have a sulk?
Wait now, I'll fix a sugar teat for you,
Unless, of course, you'd rather suck your thumb,
Brooding in your room—
　KATHLEEN.

　　　　　　　　　　I have the name!
As well to have the game!
　STANTON.

　　　　　　　　　　It's riddles, is it?
　KATHLEEN.
Riddles be damned! You think me idiotic;
I might as well fulfill your good opinion—
　　　(STANTON *walks towards her.*)
Come near me, and I'll smash your face for you.

　　　　(STANTON *embraces her.*)

　STANTON.
You're terrible fierce, you are. I wet me pants.
　KATHLEEN.
You clown, you'll spring my hairpins. Mattie, stop.
　STANTON.
Are these the hands are going to smash my face?
They're weak as white silk fans . . . I'm sorry, Kate:
You made me mad. And you know why?
　KATHLEEN.

　　　　　　　　　　　　I do.
You're as afraid as I.
　STANTON.

　　　　　　　　I am. I am.
You know me like the lashes of your eye—
　KATHLEEN.
That's more than you know me, for if you did,
You'd see what these three years have done to me—
　　　(STANTON *breaks away from her.*)
Now it's my turn to ask you where you're going.
　STANTON.
I begged you not to bring that up again.
What can I do?

KATHLEEN.
                    You can tell Father Coyne,
And ask him to apply for dispensation,
And we can be remarried secretly.

STANTON.
Now?

KATHLEEN.
        Yes, Matt, now. Before it is too late.
We aren't married.

STANTON.
                    What was that in London,
The drunkard's pledge I took?

KATHLEEN.
                        We're Catholics, Matt.
Since when can Catholics make a valid marriage
In a city hall? You have to tell the priest—

STANTON.
Shall I tell him now? Do you take me for a fool
To throw away the mayor's chair for that?

KATHLEEN.
I slink to Sunday Mass like a pavement nymph.
It's three years now since I made my Easter Duty,
Three years of telling Father Coyne that we
Receive at Easter Mass in the Cathedral,
Mortal Sin on Mortal Sin, Matt. If I died,
I'd go to Hell—

STANTON.
                    I think the woman's crazy!

KATHLEEN.
Don't you believe in God?

STANTON.
                    Of course, I do.
And more, my dear, than you who think that He
Would crush you as a man would crush a fly
Because of some mere technical mistake—

KATHLEEN.
Mere technical mistake? It's that now, is it?

A blasphemous marriage, three years' fornication,
And now presumption— Technical mistake!

(KATHLEEN *takes a cigarette out of a box on the table
    and lights it.*)

    STANTON.
I wish you wouldn't smoke them cigarettes.
High-toned though it may be in France and England,
It's a whore's habit here. (*Pause.*)
    KATHLEEN.
                  "Those cigarettes."
Don't try to hurt me, Matt. You know you can,
As I know I can you.
    STANTON.
               What do you want!
    KATHLEEN.
I want to be your wife without disgrace.
I want my honor back. I want to live
Without the need to lie. I want you to keep faith.
    STANTON.
Not now! Not now!
    KATHLEEN.
            You've said that for three years.
What is it you're afraid of?
    STANTON.
                Losing out.
You do not know these people as I do.
They turn upon the ones they make most of.
They would on me, if given half a chance.
And if it got around that we were married
In an English City Hall, lose out we would.
    KATHLEEN.
Matt, losing out? What profit for a man
To gain the world, and lose his soul?
    STANTON.
                  His soul!
That's Sunday school! That's convent folderol,

Like making half-grown girls bathe in their drawers
To put the shame of their own beauty in them,
And break their lives to bear the Church's bit.
We are not priests and nuns, but men and women.
The world religious give up is our world,
The only world we have. We have to win it
To do the bit of good we all must do;
And how are we to win the world unless
We keep the tricky rules its games are run by?
Our faith is no mere monastery faith.
It runs as fast as feeling to embrace
Whatever good it sees. And if the good
Is overgrown with bad, it still believes
God sets no traps, the bad will be cut down,
And the good push through its flowering to fruit.
Forget your convent school. Remember, Katie,
What the old women in the drowned boreens
Would say when cloudbursts beat their fields to slime,
And the potatoes blackened on their stalks
Like flesh gone proud. "Bad times is right," they'd say,
"But God is good: apples will grow again."
What sin have we committed? Marriage, Kate?
Is that a sin?

   KATHLEEN.

          It is with us.

   STANTON.

                    Because
You feel it so. It isn't. It's but prudence.
What if they should make a scandal of us?

   KATHLEEN.

Could we be worse off than we are?

   STANTON.

                    Kathleen!

   KATHLEEN.

Could we be worse off than we are, I said?

   STANTON.

Could we! We could. You don't know poverty.
You don't know what it is to do without,

Not fine clothes only, or a handsome house,
But men's respect. I do. I have been poor.
"Mattie, will you run down to the corner,
And buy me some cigars" or "Mattie, get
This gentleman a cab." Nine years, I served
Ned Quinn and Agnes Hogan, day by day,
Buying my freedom like a Roman slave.
Will you ask me to put liberty at stake
To ease your scrupulous conscience? If you do,
You're not the woman that I took you for
When I married you. Have you no courage, Kate?
    KATHLEEN.
Will you lecture me on courage? Do you dare?
When every time I walk those stairs to the street
I walk to what I know is an enemy camp.
I was not raised like you. And no offense,
Please, Mattie, no offense. I miss my home.
Whore's habit it may be to smoke, as you say,
But it brings back the talk we used to have
About old friends, new books, the Lord knows what,
On our first floor in Baggot Street in Dublin.
This following you think so much about,
We live in Mortal Sin for fear you'll lose it,
I never knew the likes of them to talk to,
Person to person. They were cooks and maids,
Or peasants at the country houses, Matt.
All they can find to talk of, servants' talk,
Serfs' talk, eternal tearing down.
I'm like a woman banished and cut off.
I've you and May in the flat downstairs. That's all.
Don't tell me I don't know what poverty is.
What bankruptcy is worse than loneliness.
They say the sense of exile is the worst
Of all the pains that torture poor damned souls.
It is that sense I live with every day.
    STANTON.
Are you the only exile of us all?
You slept your crossing through in a rosewood berth

With the swells a hundred feet below your portholes,
And ate off china on a linen cloth,
With the air around you fresh as the first of May.
I slept six deep in a bunk short as a coffin
Between a poisoned pup of a seasick boy
And a slaughtered pig of a snorer from Kildare,
Who wrestled elephants the wild nights through,
And sweated sour milk. I wolfed my meals,
Green water, and salt beef, and wooden biscuits,
On my hunkers like an ape, in a four-foot aisle
As choked as the one door of a burning school.
I crossed in mid-December: seven weeks
Of driving rain that kept the hatches battened
In a hold so low of beam a man my height
Could never lift his head. And I couldn't wash.
Water was low; the place was like an icehouse;
And girls were thick as field mice in a haystack
In the bunk across. I would have died of shame,
When I stood in the landing shed of this "promised
    land,"
As naked as the day I first saw light,
Defiled with my own waste like a dying cat,
And a lousy red beard on me like a tinker's,
While a bitch of a doctor, with his nails too long,
Dared tell me: "In Amurrica, we bathe!"
I'd have died with shame, had I sailed here to die.
I swallowed pride and rage, and made a vow
The time would come when I could spit both out
In the face of the likes of him. I made a vow
I'd fight my way to power if it killed me,
Not only for myself, but for our kind,
For the men behind me, laughing out of fear,
At their own shame as well as mine, for the women,
Behind the board partition, frightened dumb
With worry they'd be sent back home to starve
Because they'd dirty feet. I was born again.
It came to me as brutal as the cold
That makes us flinch the day the midwife takes

Our wet heels in her fist, and punches breath
Into our dangling carcasses: Get power!
Without it, there can be no decency,
No virtue and no grace. I have kept my vow.
The mayor's chair is mine but for the running.
Will you have me lose it for your convent scruples?
(*Pause.*)
KATHLEEN.
You never told me that about your landing.
STANTON.
There's many things I never told you, Kate.
I was afraid you'd hold me cheap.
KATHLEEN.

Oh, Mattie,
Don't you know me yet?
STANTON.

Stand by me.
Stand by me, Kate. The next four days count hard.
By Sunday next, I'll have won all or lost.
KATHLEEN.
What's Sunday next?
STANTON.

The Clambake for Quinn's birthday:
We're to make things up between us and make the announcement
On the steamer voyage to Seagate Sunday evening.
Stand by me, Kate. As sure as God's my judge
The minute I get into City Hall
The first thing I will do is call the priest,
And ask him to make peace with God for us.
Stand by me, Kate.
KATHLEEN.

I will though it costs my life.

(STANTON *kisses her.*)

STANTON.
God stand between us and all harm! There now!

I've wiped those words from your lips.—Oh, where's my
  mind!
I've brought champagne, and it's as warm as tears.
Go get the glasses.
> (KATHLEEN *takes two glasses down from a cup-*
> *board.* STANTON *opens the champagne and pours it.*
> *They touch glasses.*)
>   Let the past be damned,
The dead bury the dead. The future's ours.

CURTAIN

ACT I

SCENE 2

Eleven o'clock the same night. The back room of Stan-
  ton's Saloon, The Court Café. To Stage Left, glass-
  paned double doors cut the room off from the bar,
  from which a hum of VOICES can be heard. To Stage
  Right, the Ladies' Entrance. Next to it, a square
  piano with a pot of dead fern on it. Around the room,
  squat round tables and bent iron chairs. Stage Cen-
  ter, around one of the tables, with whiskeys in front
  of them, three people. At the head, JOHN "BLACK
  JACK" HAGGERTY, *in his late sixties, wearing his*
  Sunday clothes, his hair parted in the middle and
  swagged over his eyebrows in dove's wings, his han-
  dlebar mustache repeating the design. Both hair
  and mustache are dyed an improbable black. To
  HAGGERTY'S *left,* PETEY BOYLE, *a young tough in his*
  twenties, his heavy hair parted in the middle and
  combed oilily back, the teeth marks of the comb
  still in it. His rachitic frame is wiry as a weed; and
  he is dressed in a Salvation Army suit that droops
  in the seat, balloons at the knees and elbows. Next
  to BOYLE, *but facing the audience,* BESSIE LEGG, *a*
  blond girl in her late twenties or early thirties, her

hair in a pompadour under a Floradora hat that looks like an ostrich nest, a long feather boa on, together with many strands of glass beads, and rings on every finger but her thumbs, all cheap. Her doll's face is a bit crumpled, but there is no petulance in it, merely jocose self-indulgence. There is a crepe-paper shamrock tacked to the piano, and four sprung tapes of green and gold crepe paper run from the corners of the room and belly over the table in a haphazardly celebrative way.

HAGGERTY.
That Walsh from Albany was no man's fool.
The first thing that he asked about was Ag Hogan,
And then about Matt's temper, you know, the time
He nearly broke Tim Costigan in two
For calling him Hogan's Goat. But at last we cleared
  Matt.
  BOYLE.
Bess, Black Jack thinks the nomination'll stand!
  HAGGERTY.
Stop your tormenting, Petey. Of course, it will.
Amn't I Assistant Leader of this Ward
And head of the Matthew Stanton Association?
And isn't Palsy Murphy Boss of Brooklyn
And head of the Edward Quinn Association?
Walsh said that Father Coyne and the both of us
Would constitute a due and legal caucus;
And he's the representative of the Party,
He ought to know.
  BESSIE.
                    Yeah? When does Quinn find out?
  HAGGERTY.
Tomorrow morning. It has to be told him fast.
We're to break the news Matt's nominated Sunday
At the Clambake for Quinn's birthday down in Seagate.
  BOYLE.
Is both Associations going on this Clambake?

HAGGERTY.
Yes. Murphy's got the job of telling Quinn
And getting him to make things up with Matt.
   BOYLE.
That's a moonlight voyage we'll all be seeing stars.
It'll make the riot on the *Harvest Queen,*
When that Alderman knifed that guy in '87,
Look like a slapping match in St. Mary's schoolyard.
Quinn ain't never giving up to no Stanton
In no four days.
   BESSIE.
                    Dust off your steel derby,
Or your head will be all lumps like a bag of marbles.
   BOYLE.
You tell him, kid. I'll hold the baby.
   HAGGERTY.
                                        Lord!
What a pair of lochremauns! That's why Murphy's Boss:
He could talk a Hindu out of a tiger's mouth.
He'll find some cosy way to break the news,
And Quinn will purr like a kitten.

(*Enter* MARIA HAGGERTY *through the Ladies' Entrance.
    She is a tall, raw-boned woman in her late sixties,
    with loose-stranded iron-gray hair pulled back around
    a center part in a tight bun. She wears a rusty black
    toque, and a long black woolen coat with a frayed
    hem, and is carrying a large handbag, which she sets
    down on the floor as she settles wearily into the chair
    to Stage Right of* HAGGERTY, *her husband.*)

   MARIA.
                              Ah, there you are!
How are you, Mrs. Legg? How are you, Petey?
I thought you might be waiting here for Matt,
When Josie told me. Why is it so secret?
   HAGGERTY.
It won't be secret long with Josie Finn

Trumpeting it from here to Fulton Ferry
Like an elephant in heat. Quinn doesn't know yet.
That's why it's so secret.
MARIA.

                    What's that you're drinking?

HAGGERTY.
Whiskey and water, May.
MARIA.

                    Give Ma a swallow.

HAGGERTY.
Great God in Heaven, drink it all, why don't you!
We're met to celebrate Matt Stanton's luck.
Corner-boy Boyle and Bessie the balloon brain
See trouble in store undreamed by Albany,
And my wife drags in here with a puss on her
Like a lead-horse on a hearse. What's the matter with
    you?
MARIA.
I'm sure I'm glad for Matt's sake. He's worked hard,
And he's been good, giving us the flat and all.
But in a way, you know, Ned Quinn is right:
Matt's hard on people, harder than he should be.
He's a lot to answer for before he dies.
BESSIE.
You mean Ag Hogan?
MARIA.

                    Yes, I do.

BESSIE.

                    Poor girl.
When I was there this morning, she looked awful.
MARIA.
She'll never live to comb out a gray head.
I've just now come from giving her her tea,
In that coffin of a furnished room in Smith Street.
I looked at the cheesecloth curtains hung on strings;
And I thought of all those velvet-muffled windows,
Those carpets red as blood and deep as snow,

Those tables glistening underneath the lamps
Like rosy gold, in her big house in Seagate.
And I said to myself, if it weren't for Agnes Hogan,
Matt would be a grocery clerk at Nolan's,
And not the owner of The Court Café.
And candidate for mayor; and there she lies,
Flat on her back with two beanbags of buckshot
On her shriveled breasts, to chain her to the mattress,
As if she could move, her eyes in a black stare
At the white paint peeling off that iron bedstead,
Like scabs of a rash; and he never once comes near her,
For fear, I suppose, they'd call him Hogan's Goat,
And his missis might find out about their high jinks.
And yet if Matt were any kind of man,
Wouldn't he go and take her in his arms,
And say, "You hurt me bad three years ago;
But I hurt you as bad. Forgive and forget."
Maybe it's because the girl's my niece,
But I think I'd feel the same if she were not.

    HAGGERTY.

Be that as may be, what has passed between them
Is their affair. It isn't ours to judge,
Especially after all Matt's done for us—
And you'll set this one thinking how Tom Legg
Left her in the lurch in Baltic Street,
And spraying us all like a drainpipe in a downpour,
If you keep up that way. Sure, what's past is past.
What can't be remedied must be endured.

    BESSIE.

Say, listen here, Napoleon the Turd,
Legg never found me in no bed with no one,
Like Matt done Ag, if that's what you're implying.

    HAGGERTY.

How could he, when he worked in the subway nights,
And was so blind he couldn't tie his shoes
Without his nose to the eyelets, his rump in the air,
Like a startled ostrich.

    BESSIE.

              Say that again, I dare you!

HAGGERTY.
No matter now. It served what it was meant to:
Better glares than tears—

(*A loud SHOUT from the bar. APPLAUSE, CHEERS
and SINGING. Enter* STANTON *from the bar with a*
CROWD *around him, singing. The* FOUR *at the table
join in.*)

EVERYBODY.
He'll make a jolly good mayor!
He'll make a jolly good mayor!
He'll make a jolly good mayor!
Which nobody can deny!
HAGGERTY.
Speech, Mattie, speech!
STANTON.
                          Thanks all! What will I say!
It's me who should be singing songs to you,
Not you to me. And I don't know how you've learned
That I'm to run for mayor. It's a secret.
Ask the man who told you if it isn't,
Jack Haggerty— (*Applause.*)
                          When I returned from England
Three years ago with my new wife, I thought
My chances to get back into the Party
Were gone for good. Yet in those three short years
You stuck by me so fast, the Party made me
Leader of the Ward in which the mayor
I had a falling-out with lives; and now
You're bent on giving me his place.
Ned Quinn—

(*BOOING and HISSING.* PETEY BOYLE *jumps on a table, puts one fist on his hip, throws his head back
insolently, and sings, in a nasal imitation of John
McCormack. Enter* FATHER COYNE, *unnoticed,
through the Ladies' Entrance, wearing his biretta
and an old black overcoat shorter than his cassock.*)

BOYLE.
Is it Ned Quinn you mean? } (*Repeat.*)
Says the Shan Van Vocht,
He's in Fogarty's shebeen
Drinking bourbon with some quean, (*Repeat.*)
Says the Shan Van Vocht.
Let him drink it to the dregs, } (*Repeat.*)
Says the Shan Van Vocht.
For the goose that lays gold eggs
Lays no more for hollow legs, (*Repeat.*)
Says the Shan Van Vocht.

(*APPLAUSE and LAUGHTER.* BOYLE *motions for silence and sings.*)

BOYLE.
Go and tell that swindler!

(BOYLE *points to* HAGGERTY.)

HAGGERTY.
Go and tell that swindler!

(HAGGERTY *points to* BESSIE.)

BESSIE.
Go and tell that swindler!
BOYLE.
What the Shan Van Vocht has said!

(BOYLE *apes a choir director.*)

EVERYBODY.
What the Shan Van Vocht has said!

(*LAUGHTER and APPLAUSE.* FATHER COYNE *angrily jostles his way to Stage Center, the* PEOPLE *shamefacedly making way for him.*)

FATHER COYNE.
For shame! For shame! Have you no charity?
Don't turn upon the man, but on his sin.
   HAGGERTY.
Father! Sit down. I thought you'd be in bed.
   FATHER COYNE.
I couldn't sleep. I thought I'd come by here
And have a word with Matt alone.
   BOYLE.

                       A word or a drink?

   FATHER COYNE.
What's that you say, Pete Boyle? Speak up, why don't
   you,
And show them how malicious you can be,
And you so drunk!
   BOYLE.
              I didn't mean no harm.

   FATHER COYNE.
You meant no harm! You're all of you alike.
You talk to preen your wit or flex your pride,
Not to lay bare your hearts or tell God's truth.
Words have more force than blows. They can destroy.
Would you punch an old man's face to test your arm?
Answer me, Pete Boyle.
   BOYLE.
               You know I wouldn't.

   FATHER COYNE.
You did as much to me.
   BOYLE.

               I'm sorry, Father.

   FATHER COYNE.
I hope you are, my son. Don't look so pious,
The rest of you. You're just as bad as him,
Dancing around the ruin of Quinn's name
Like a pack of savages. Do you know the story
The Rabbis set down centuries ago
Beside the part in Exodus where the Jews
Are shown exulting over the drowned troops

Of Pharaoh on the shores of the Red Sea?
The angels, says the story, joined their voices
With those of the men below. And God cried out:
"What reason is there to hold jubilee?
The men of Egypt are my children too!"
The men of Egypt were God's enemies,
And Edward Quinn's your friend, may God forgive you!

    STANTON.

That kind of justice is too heavenly
For us on earth. If we condone Ned Quinn,
Don't we condone corruption with him, Father?

    FATHER COYNE.

You know, don't you, a man can commit theft,
And yet not be a thief by nature, Matt?
Corruption sometimes saps the choicest men;
Sometimes it is disordered sweetness drives
A man to act contrary to what's right.
Collusion can arise from faithfulness,
And graft from bankrupt generosity.
You know I'd never ask you to condone that.
But once he's made the city restitution,
The loss of office is enough chastisement
For Edward Quinn. You must not banish him.
What purpose would it serve to break a man
Who's slaved for Church and people thirty years?

    STANTON.

What purpose would it serve? 'Twould end corruption.
Corruption, Father, may be, as you say,
Disordered sweetness sometimes, but in men
Who govern others, can we risk disorder
To save the heart it works its ferment on?
A man may cut away the seething bruise
That festers in good fruit or even flesh.
The heart's corruption poisons surgery.
The pulse of it is rapid. It pollutes
Like ratbite, and like ratbite spawns
Plagues to charge whole graveyards.
Isolate its carriers fast, I say. Disown them,

Before they can infect us with the pox
We came across the ocean to avoid,
Liberty gone blind, the death of honor! —
Would you have the big men of this city say
That they were right in keeping us cheap labor,
Because we are not fit for nobler service,
We dirty what we touch? Say that they will,
And with full right, unless we dare cut free
From these enfeebling politics of pity,
And rule the city right. Ned Quinn must go—-

(*APPLAUSE.*)

HAGGERTY.
Hurray for Stanton! The man is right, God bless him.
What answer, Father, can you make to that?
    FATHER COYNE.
What answer, Black Jack, but the same old answer?
Judge not, Matt Stanton, lest yourself be judged;
Beware, Matt Stanton, lest in pointing out
The mote within your neighbor's watering eye,
You overlook the beam that blinds your own.
    STANTON.
I meant no disrespect. Forgive me, Father.
    FATHER COYNE.
Do not delude yourself it is offense
Has made me quote the Scripture to you, man.
I dare not take offense. My task is love.
I have no passion save the one for souls.
Salus suprema lex, remember that,
Salvation is the law that must come first.
My cure includes both you and Edward Quinn.
Because it does, I have to warn you, Matt,
Do not mistake vindictiveness for justice.
I hope you take my meaning. Do you?
    STANTON.
                                        Yes.
I'll make no move against Ned Quinn, I promise,
Unless he moves against me first.

FATHER COYNE.

Good, Matt.

STANTON.

For your penance, Petey, draw the priest a beer.

FATHER COYNE.

I won't tonight, Matt, thank you. I've a matter
I'd like to talk to you about alone.

STANTON.

Sure, Father— Out, the lot of you, to the bar.
The drinks are on the house.

HAGGERTY.

Stanton abu, boys.

BOYLE.

Let the Jickies and the Prods,
Says the Shan Van Vocht,
Look down on us like gods,
Says the Shan Van Vocht.
We've got Stanton, damn the odds,
Says the Shan Van Vocht.

(*Exit* EVERYBODY *cheering. Pause.*)

FATHER COYNE.

It's no good being delicate. If I tried,
I'd put your eye out, Matt, or break your bones.
I'll just come out and say it: go see Ag.

STANTON.

Agnes Hogan, Father?

FATHER COYNE.

Agnes Hogan.

What other Ag would I mean?

STANTON.

I can't do that.

FATHER COYNE.

You can't or you won't?

STANTON.

One knock at Aggie's door,
And Josie Finn would be scissoring down Fifth Place

With the wind in tatters around her, and at Kate's ear
Before the latch was lifted. It would all come out—
    FATHER COYNE.
It should have come out long since. Ag's dying, Matt.
Tell Kate about her, and go.
    STANTON.

                    Whose fault she's dying?
Did you ever know her stop when the thirst was on her?
Who poured that whiskey down her fourteen months
Until the lungs were tattered in her breast?
Who landed her in Saranac? (*Pause.*)
                    She was always like that.
Whiskey, or clothes, or diamonds . . . or men!
You can say what you want of Joe Finn and her tongue,
If it wasn't for her, I'd never have found out
I was the goat for fair.
    FATHER COYNE.

              Ag was fully clothed.
And so was Quinn.
    STANTON.

             You didn't see them, Father.
They were leg in leg when Josie brought me in.
Asleep, I grant you, but his ham of a hand
Was tangled in the fullness of her hair—
    FATHER COYNE.
You told me that long since. What's done is done.
Don't let the woman die unreconciled.
Tell Kate, and go to see her.
    STANTON.

                Yes, but—
    FATHER COYNE.

                    What?
What can I know of love, a celibate,
Numb as a broomstick in my varnished parlor,
With my frightened curate jumping at each word,
And Ann Mulcahy to do my housekeeping
Without a whimper of complaint? What can I know?
Putting aside the fact that priesthood's marriage

To a Partner Who is always right, I know
If you don't tell Kate, there are others will,
Before the ink is dry on the campaign posters,
And that would be disastrous—

STANTON.

Tell her what!

FATHER COYNE.
Don't take that tone with me.

STANTON.

I lived with her?
Shall I tell my wife I serviced Ag three years?

FATHER COYNE.
If you're trying to shock me, Matt, you're being simple.
For forty years, no Saturday's gone by,
I have not sat alone from three to nine
In my confessional, and heard men spill
Far blacker things than that. Man, use your reason!

STANTON.
I loved Ag, and kept faith.

FATHER COYNE.

Who says you didn't?

STANTON.
I loved her and kept faith. I did my part.
She played me false with Quinn.

FATHER COYNE.

If you loved her, Matt,
How is it that you didn't marry her,
Before she, how did you put it, played you false? (*Pause.*)

STANTON.
Not to give you a short answer, Father,
But don't you think that's my affair?

FATHER COYNE.

No, Matt.

STANTON.
It's not the kind of thing you talk to priests of.

FATHER COYNE.
You're trying to make me angry, aren't you?
Since *you* won't tell *me* why, let me tell you.

You only wanted Ag for fun and games;
You didn't want her on your neck for life.
You thought she'd spoil your chances, didn't you?
Your chances for the mayor's chair? You thought,
If you married her, they'd call you Hogan's Goat
To the day you died. Your heart rejoiced when you
    found
The both of them in bed—
    STANTON.

                      Are you finished, Father?
    FATHER COYNE.
No, Matt. I'm not. Do you know why you're fuming?
Because you're a good man, and you feel ashamed,
Because I'm saying what you tell yourself:
Whatever wrong was done was on both sides.
The woman made you what you are today;
The woman's dying. Hogan's Goat, or not,
Pocket your pride, and tell your wife about her.
Go talk with Ag, and let her die in peace,
Or else you'll be her goat in the Bible sense,
With all her sins on your head, and the world a desert.
Do you think I like to say such things to you?
I'm trying to help you, Matt.
    STANTON.

                     I had the right
To show her no one plays Matt Stanton false
More than one time!
    FATHER COYNE.

                If you'd the right, my son,
Why are you screaming at me?
    STANTON.

                  Because you'd have me
Destroy this new life I've been three years building,
Not only for myself but for my kind,
By dragging my poor wife to the room in my heart
Where my dead loves are waked. (*Pause.*)
    FATHER COYNE.

                    Tell Kathleen, Matt.

Maybe it's that which stands between you, son,
And stiffens both your backs against each other.
    STANTON.
Who dares to say that something stands between us?
That's a pack of lies!
    FATHER COYNE.

                Is it? Tell Katie, Matt—

    (BOYLE *bursts through the bar door.*)

    BOYLE.
It's Aggie Hogan, Father.
She's dying; and she won't confess to your curate.
They want you.
    FATHER COYNE.
            Mattie?
    STANTON.

              Sacred Heart of Jesus!

    FATHER COYNE.
Will you come with me?
    STANTON.
              I will, Father. I will.

    (*Exit all* THREE *through the Ladies' Entrance.*)

          CURTAIN

ACT I

SCENE 3

*Midnight the same night. The all-night Printers' Church
in the Newspaper Row of Brooklyn on lower Fulton
Street.* STANTON *kneels on a prie-dieu with a framed
baize curtain atop it.* FATHER MALONEY *sits on the
other side of the prie-dieu, hearing his Confession.*

    STANTON.
Bless me, Father. I have sinned. Three years.

It is three years since I made my last Confession.
I accuse myself of lying many times.

FATHER MALONEY.

How many times?

STANTON.

                 God knows!

FATHER MALONEY.

                       With a mind to harm?

STANTON.

God knows!

FATHER MALONEY.

            Take hold of yourself. What ails you!

STANTON.

I did a woman wrong. Tonight she died.
Tomorrow is her wake.

FATHER MALONEY.

                  What kind of wrong

Is it you did her?

STANTON.

          I . . .

FATHER MALONEY.

                  What kind of wrong?

STANTON.

I lived with her three years before I married.
They pulled the sheet over her face an hour ago.
The hem of it gave. It was gray as a buried rag.
She wouldn't have the priest. She lay there sweating,
And they around her with their lighted candles.
She glowered and said, "If such love was a sin,
I'd rather not make peace with God at all."
They pressed her hard. She shook and shook her head.
She kept on shaking it until she died—
Absolve her through me!

FATHER MALONEY.

                 You know I can't do that.

STANTON.

What can you do then!

FATHER MALONEY.

                 Absolve *you* from *your* sin.

STANTON.

Her sin is mine. Absolve the both of us.

FATHER MALONEY.

Why did you leave this woman?

STANTON.

She played me false.

I found her in the one bed with a man—
She stood on the wide porch with her hair down, crying.
I walked away. I heard her screaming at me.
She told me, go, yes go, but not to come back. Never.
She'd rip the clothes she bought me into threads
And throw them in the fire. She'd burn my letters,
And every bit of paper that I'd put my name to.
And she did . . . I'm sure she did. She was wild by nature.
But tonight . . . when I came back . . . she stretched out her hands
Like a falling child . . .

FATHER MALONEY

Go on.

STANTON.

And I turned away—

I cannot rest with thinking of her face
And that black look of stubborn joy on it.

FATHER MALONEY.

Well for you, you can't rest. She died in the Devil's arms
In a glory of joy at the filthy shame to her flesh
You visited on her, and like all the rest,
You come to a strange priest outside your parish
In the mistaken hope he will not judge you,
But give you comfort when you need correction.
What about this other one you took up with
When you threw the dead one over?—

STANTON.

Jesus, Father!

FATHER MALONEY.

Don't take the name of the Lord in vain to me!

STANTON.

I don't know why I came here in the first place.

FATHER MALONEY.

You came here for forgiveness—

STANTON.

From the likes of you!
For thirty years I've put up with your kind.
Since my First Communion. Saturday Confession!
Spayed mutts of men, born with no spice of pride,
Living off the pennies of the poor,
Huddled in their fat in basement booths,
Calling the true vaulting of the heart
Towards its desire filth and deviation,
Dragging me, and all unlike you down—·

FATHER MALONEY.

Whatever a noble creature like yourself
May think of me, I'm here to do God's work;
And since that begins with dragging you down to the
     earth
We all have come from and must all return to,
Drag you down I will. God lifts none but the humble—

STANTON.

The pride steams off you like the stink of cancer,
And you sit there and preach humility!

FATHER MALONEY.

Take care! I will deny you absolution.

STANTON.

What harm! Who can absolve us but ourselves!
I am what I am. What I have done, I'd cause for.
It was seeing what life did to her unmanned me;
It was looking in her eyes as they guttered out
That drove me here like a scared kid from the bogs
Who takes the clouds that bruise the light for demons.
But thanks to the words from the open grave of your
     mouth
I see that fear for the wind in fog that it is
And it is killed for good. I'm my own man now.
I can say that for the first time in my life.

I'm free of her; and I'm free of you and yours.
Come what come may to me, from this day forward,
I'll not fall to my knees for man or God.

(STANTON *rises, and quickly strides out.* FATHER MA-
    LONEY *rises.*)

    FATHER MALONEY.
Will you dare to turn your back on the living God!

CURTAIN

ACT I

SCENE 4

*Ten o'clock, Friday morning, April 29, 1890. The back
    room of Fogarty's Saloon.* JAMES "PALSY" MURPHY
    *sits at a chair pushed well back from a table, appre-
    hensively holding a sheaf of papers in his hand. He
    is a florid, rather stout man in his late fifties, with
    black hair* en brosse, *graying at the temples.* MAYOR
    EDWARD QUINN *stands facing* MURPHY *like a statue
    of a lawyer in a park. He is a tall, husky, big-boned
    man in his seventies, bald, but with hair growing out
    of his ears. He is dressed in rumpled morning clothes.*

    QUINN.
Does Matthew Stanton think he can oust me
By hole-in-corner meetings in school halls,
With craw thumpers and Sunday-pass-the-plates,
Black Jack the plug and the ga-ga Parish Priest
Both nodding yes to everything he says
Like slobbering dummies?—What is it that he said?
    MURPHY.
Do you want to hear?
    QUINN.
                    Would I ask, James, if I didn't?

MURPHY.
Listen then. I have . . . full notes on it.
I took down everything that Stanton said.
    QUINN.
Read it. Read it. Do you want applause?
    MURPHY.
No, Ned: attention. Here: "My dear old friends,
When Father Coyne asked me to speak to you,
He said it was about Ag Hogan's bills,
A gathering to help raise funds to pay them.
I never thought the purpose of this meeting
Would be political"—
    QUINN.
               "I never thought
The purpose of this meeting"—Father Coyne!
I roofed his sieve of a church and glazed it too;
And put a tight new furnace in its cellar.
There's not a priest you can trust!
    MURPHY.
Will you listen, Ned!
    QUINN.
               I'm listening. Go on.
    MURPHY.
"The Party of Reform"—
    QUINN.
"The Party of Reform"! Ah, yes, reform!
A Lutheran lawyer with a flytrap mouth
And a four-bit practice of litigious Swedes
In a closet rank as rats down by the river!
A lecherous broker with a swivel eye
You wouldn't trust with Grandma in a hack!
A tear-drawers arm in arm with a gaping bollocks!
    MURPHY.
Will you quit your interrupting!
    QUINN.
               Read on. Read on.

MURPHY.
"The Party of Reform has in its hands
Sworn affidavits on the city books"—
   QUINN.
Got by collusion and by audits forged
As the certificates above their parents' beds!—
   MURPHY.
"The Party of Reform has in its hands
Sworn affidavits on the city books,
Drawn up from careful audit, and declaring
A hidden deficit of fifteen thousand"—
   QUINN.
Of fifteen thousand! The unfortunates!
They couldn't even get that business right.
It's twenty thousand, Palsy, if it's a cent! (*Glum pause.*)
I'm in the treasury for twenty thousand. (*Pause.*)
   MURPHY.
"You say they will expose us to the public,
Unless we guarantee that Edward Quinn
Resigns as candidate in the next election"—
   QUINN.
See, that's Matt's game. He's out to get my job;
But he's not the guts to grab it like a man.
Will you listen to the cagey way he puts it:
"*You* say *they* will expose *us* to the public!"
As sneaky as a rat in a hotel kitchen.
Don't you see the cunning of it, James? The craft?
It's not my job he wants, but to save the Party!
And all I did for him. I made him, James.
I picked him up when he first came to me,
Twelve years ago, when he was twenty-five
And lost his job for beating up that grocer.
He'd no knees in his pants; his coat was slick
With grease as a butcher's thumb. He was skin and bones.
I was sitting here in Fogarty's back room,
With poor Ag Hogan codding me, when he
Burst in the door, and asked me for my help.

"I'll do anything that's honest, Mr. Quinn,"
Is what he says. He had that crooked grin—
It reminded me of Patrick that's long dead,
Patrick, my poor brother—

MURPHY.

                   Go on, now, Ned!
Leave out the soft-soap. He'd a crooked grin
You knew would serve you well among the women—

QUINN.

I should have said, "Go now, and scare the crows,
Raggedy-arse Keho; that's all you're good for!"
But, no, there was that grin; and Ag said, "Take him."
She loved him, the poor slob, from the day she saw him,
Fat good it did her. "You can put him on
With Judge Muldooney," says she; "take him, Ned,
God will bless us for it . . ." (*Pause.*)

                   Aggie's dead, James. Dead.

MURPHY.

Yes, Ned. She is.

QUINN.

                Did Stanton get to see her? (*Pause.*)
Did he?

MURPHY.

        Yes.

QUINN.

             She wouldn't let me in. (*Pause.*)

MURPHY.

I'm sorry, Ned.

QUINN.

             And Stanton's high-toned wife?
What did she say when she found out about them?

MURPHY.

She didn't, Ned. She knows that Ag helped Matt,
But nothing else.

QUINN.

             Ah, nothing else? I see.
Where was I, Palsy?

MURPHY.
                    "All I done for him,"
Fifth book, tenth chapter—
    QUINN.
                        Go to hell, James Murphy.
You think it's funny, do you? I'll give you fun.
If it's jail for me, you know, it's jail for you.
No hundred-dollar suits and fancy feeds
With tarts in Rector's drinking cold champagne
From glasses bright as ice with hollow stems,
But tea from yellowed cups and mulligan
Foul as the odds and ends they make it from.
    MURPHY.
Sure, they'll send us puddings.
    QUINN.
                        Are you mad, or what?
I tell you, I'm in danger. I'm in danger.
Don't shake your head. They're spoiling for the kill.
It's in their blood.
    MURPHY.
                    Whose blood?
    QUINN.
                        Whose blood but our own.
They turn upon the strong, and pull them down,
And not from virtue, James, but vicious pride.
They want to hold their heads up in this city,
Among the members of the Epworth League,
The Church of Ethical Culture and the Elks,
That's why they're taking sides with Ole Olson,
Or whatever the hell his name is, and that whore
From Wall Street in the clean pince-nez. For thirty years
I've kept their heads above the water, James,
By fair means or by foul. Now they've reached the shore
They'd rather not remember how they got there.
They want to disown me. They're a faithless lot,
And Matthew Stanton is the worst of all--
Read on, why don't you? What's the matter with you?
    (Pause.)

MURPHY.
"I would not stand in this school hall before you
If Edward Quinn had not, in his full power,
Made of me what I am. I cannot think,
Since you have shared his generosity
As long as I, that you are asking me
To help you pull him down"—
            QUINN.

                                    Good Jesus, James!
        MURPHY.
"The way to cope with the Party of Reform's
To raise the funds to make Quinn's deficit up.
I pledge three thousand dollars, and I ask
Each and every one of you who can
To give as much as possible. Ned Quinn
Must not live out his final days in jail
Because he was too kindly to be wise"—
            QUINN.
I want no handouts from the likes of him.
Will he pity me?
        MURPHY.
                        What's that?
        QUINN.

                                    You heard me, James.
Will he pity me? Does he think I need his pity!
I made him, and I can unmake him too,
And make another in his place. I'm old,
I'm far too old to live on charity
From a greenhorn that I picked up in a barroom
To run my sweetheart's errands. Don't you see, James?
He took Ag from me first; that's how he started.
He ran her roadhouse for her. "He was handsome!
He'd skin like milk, and eyes like stars in winter!"
And he was young and shrewd! She taught him manners:
What clothes to wear, what cutlery to begin with,
What twaddle he must speak when introduced
To the state bigwigs down from Albany.
He told her that he loved her. She ditched me.

I'm twenty years her senior. Then that day,
That famous Labor Day three years ago,
We'd a drink or two, you know, for old times' sake,
And we passed out, and that bitch Josie Finn
Found out about us, and brought Matt in on us,
Our arms around each other like two children.
And he spat on poor Ag's carpet, called her a whore,
Me a degenerate. Three years ago,
The very year he married this Kathleen,
The Lord knows who, James, from the Christ knows where,
In some cosy hocus-pocus there in London,
To show Ag he could do without her. He never spoke
To Ag at all until he found her done for,
Dying lung by lung. He'd never speak to me at all
If I were not in trouble.
Don't you see the triumph of it, Palsy Murphy!
He takes his vengeance in a show of mercy.
He weeps as he destroys! He's a crocodile—
    MURPHY.
Ned, I . . .
    QUINN.
            Ned what?
    MURPHY.
                    I hope you won't be hurt.
We on the Party board agree with Matt.
We feel the time has come for some new blood—
    QUINN.
"We on the Party board agree with Matt"!
Now it comes out at last! It all comes out!
You and your pack of lies, your trumped-up story,
Pretending to be reading what he said
When you can't read a thing that hasn't pictures.
Did you think me such a boob I wouldn't know
What you and Walsh were up to here last night?
It made the rounds of the Ward by half past nine!
    (Pause.)
Bismarck the diplomat! You goddamned fool,

Pouring that vat of soft-soap over me!
"Because he was too kindly to be wise"!
They'll soon be making you the editor
Of *The Messenger of the Sacred Heart*.
    MURPHY.

                                Now, Ned—
    QUINN.
"Now, Ned." "Now, Ned." Shut up, or I'll drink your
    blood.
The only thing rang true in what you said
Was Stanton's offer to be noble to me. (*Pause.*)
    MURPHY.
I wanted to break it easy. Matt made no offer.
The Party it is will cover you on the books.
But on one condition, Ned: you must resign.
    QUINN.
I must resign. We'll see who backs out first.
I didn't stay the mayor of this city
For thirty years by taking orders, James.
You tell the Party board I'll rot in prison
Before I'll let Matt Stanton take my place.
You tell the Party board I'll meet the debits
The Party of Reform found in the books.
You tell the Party board they'd best not cross me.
Don't look as if you think this all is blather.
There's not a one of you I can't get at,
You least of all. Remember that, James Murphy.
How long, do you think, that knowing what I know
About your money, James, and how you got it,
The Jesuit Fathers at St. Francis Xavier's,
With all their bon-ton notions of clean hands,
Would let your boys play soldier in their yard?
Don't glare like that at me. You tell the board
What I have said. I meant it, every word.
    MURPHY.
The Party will disown you!
    QUINN.
                                Let them try!

I'll grease the palm of every squarehead deadbeat
From Greenwood Cemetery to the Narrows
Who'll stagger to the polls for three months' rent,
I'll buy the blackface vote off all the fences
Down Fulton Street from Hudson Avenue.
I'll vote from every plot in Holy Cross
With an Irish headstone on it. I'll win this fight—
   MURPHY.
I'll telegraph to Albany. I warn you!
   QUINN.
Damn Albany! Get out of here. Get out!
     (*Exit* MURPHY *Stage Left.* QUINN *walks over to the bar door to Stage Right.*)
Hey, Bill.
     (*Enter* BILL, *a wiry bowlegged man about seventy who has the look of a drunk.*)
     Go down to one-o-seventy Luqueer Street,
And get me Josie Finn— On second thought,
Best wait till noon and collar me some schoolboy
To run the errand for me. If they saw you,
They'd know 'twas I that wanted her. And yes!
Send to Fitzsimmons and Rooney for a wreath,
A hundred-dollar wreath, and have them spell
This message out in them gold-paper letters
On a silk-gauze band: "For Agnes Mary Hogan,
Gone but not forgotten." Look alive!

CURTAIN

ACT I

SCENE 5

Eight o'clock the same evening. The Haggertys' kitchen, beneath the Stantons' parlor in the double set. The kitchen table and chairs are of cheap oak, varnished and revarnished until they look charred and blistered. The chairs are unmatched, and of the "Queen

Anne" style, jerry-built replicas of a bad idea of eighteenth-century furniture, with die-embossed designs on the back, their seats repaired with pressed cardboard. Behind the table stands the big coal cooking stove, jammed into the chimney. The mantelpiece is covered with newspaper cut into daggers of rough lace and filled with every kind of souvenir you could think of, yellowing letters, bills, clippings stuck behind the grimy ornaments. To Stage Right of the stove, an entrance into the three remaining rooms of the flat, an opening hung with a single portiere of heavy, warped, faded brown velour on greasy wooden rings. Through that opening, from time to time, as the scene progresses, can be heard the sound of PEOPLE saying the Rosary. The door of the flat, giving on the hall and the stairs to the Stantons' flat, is ajar; and leaned against it glitters Edward Quinn's appalling flower piece. Seated to Stage Left of the table is JOSIE FINN, a tall, rather handsome woman in her late thirties, with her black hair in a loose bun. Opposite her sits ANN MULCAHY, a small, plump woman with a face like a withered apple, red hair gone white, and fine searching eyes. Between them, its back to the audience, stands an empty chair. They have cups in front of them, and are waiting for the kettle to boil for the tea.

ANN.
I'm sure Matt will have luck for burying Ag
And letting Maisie hold the wake downstairs here
In his own house for all that past between them.

(JOSIE nods disconsolately. Enter PETEY BOYLE, swaying slightly, his hat in his hands.)

BOYLE.
I'm sorry for your trouble, Mrs. Finn.
JOSIE.
My trouble, Petey. Trouble it is for fair.

That's Aggie Hogan that's laid out in there,
My dead aunt's daughter, that I haven't talked to
For, Mother of God, I think it's three long years
September.
    BOYLE.
                If you come to crow about it,
My ass on you then, kid—
    JOSIE.
                     Sir, you presume!

John Haggerty!

(BOYLE *scurries through the portiere to the sanctuary of
the coffin.*)

    ANN.
Now don't be calling Jack. It will cause trouble.
Poor Petey Boyle was always ignorant.
He meant no harm by talking to you dirty,
Josie dear.
    JOSIE.
            It's not his talking dirty
Made me mad. What kind of creature must he take me for,
To come to crow at my own cousin's wake!—
You know, Ag wouldn't see me at the last?
    ANN.
Nor would she have the priest. She was crazed with pain,
In fever tantrums, don't you know, half dead.
She hardly knew what she was doing.
    JOSIE.
Ann, you're a saint.
    ANN.
              Now, Josie, praise is poison,
Though I thank you for the kindness that's behind it.
    JOSIE.
How can you live, remembering what you've done,
Unless you are a saint, or a half brute,
Like Quinn in there!

ANN.
                       By doing what you must;
And begging for the grace to forgive yourself
As well as others when you don't do right.
You just reminded me: I hope Ned's going soon.
It's getting on towards eight; and Matt's expected down.
    JOSIE.
Oh, Quinn knows that. Sure, Quinn knows everything:
Whose money's stained, and how, and whose is not;
Who's in whose bed, and who is not, and why;
Who has a shame to hide that he can use
To coat his nest with slime against the wind!
    ANN.
There's a bit of skunk in all of us, you know.
We stink when we're afraid or hurt. Ned's both.
    JOSIE.
Pray for me, Ann Mulcahy. I've made a vow
On my dead mother's grave to guard my tongue
And keep my temper.
    ANN.
                      God in Heaven help you.
    JOSIE.
It's up to me, not Him.
    ANN.
                    Ah, don't say that.
Sure, that's presumption.
    JOSIE.
                   Then I won't say that.
But thinking back on things I've said and done,
And my knees all bunions, kneeling out novenas,
If you think that God and all His holy angels
Can shut my mouth once anger oils the hinges,
You're more a fool than ever I took you for
When first I met you—

(*Enter* FATHER COYNE, *dressed in the same rusty black
coat and frayed biretta.*)

FATHER COYNE.

             Here in the nick of time!
Who's calling my lost parish's one saint
A fool to her face!

JOSIE.

          Good evening to you, Father.

FATHER COYNE.
Good evening, Mrs. Finn. I'm glad to see
Your three hard years of war with the deceased
Has ended in some show of gallantry.
What was the fight about? Do you recall?

JOSIE.
You well know that I do. But what's been has been.
She'd have done the same for me.

FATHER COYNE.

            I'm sure she would:
For where would be the harm in that, I ask you?
There'd be small danger of much conversation
To thaw your icy hearts—

ANN.

            Please, Father Coyne—

FATHER COYNE.
Dear God, forgive me. I forgot you, Ann.
It's like me to fly out at Mrs. Finn
With the one soul left here I could scandalize
From Dwight Street to the steps of City Hall.
I'll be as gracious as St. Francis Sales
To make it up to you, Ann— Now, Mrs. Finn,
And how have you been ever since?

JOSIE.

            Since when?

FATHER COYNE.
Since Easter Sunday three long years ago,
The last time that I saw you in my church!

JOSIE.
There's other churches!

FATHER COYNE.

                     Yes, but not this parish;
And that's where you belong—
    (ANN *touches* FATHER COYNE *on the sleeve and
    looks into his eyes.*)
                      I'm a sinful man.
Pray for me, Ann Mulcahy. I'll begin the beads,
Before I throw my forty years of prayer
Into the pits of Hell to best a slanderer.
Will you come with me?
    ANN.

                      In a minute, Father.
The kettle's on the boil.

    (*Exit* FATHER COYNE *through the portiere. Pause.*)

    JOSIE.

                      I have the name;
As well to have the game!
    ANN.

                      He meant no harm.
He's torn apart with trying to talk sense
To poor Ag dying; and he struck at you
Because you brought the days back Ag was well. (*Pause.*)
Will you wet the tea, while I go in and ask
If Ned Quinn can't be hurried just a bit.
I'm destroyed with worrying that Matt will come.

(*Exit* ANN. *Sound of ROSARY.* JOSIE *rises, and brews
    the tea in a large earthenware pot. Enter* QUINN
    quietly through the portiere. Sound of ROSARY.
    JOSIE *looks up from the stove, directly at him, then
    away. Most of their conversation is carried on with
    averted faces.*)

    QUINN.
Why have they put that wedding ring on Ag? (*Pause.*)
    JOSIE.
She asked them to. She said it was her mother's. (*Pause.*)

QUINN.

What harm would there be in it, I'd like to know!

JOSIE.

You'd like to know? You know damned well what harm.
I told you no this afternoon. I meant it.
Am I your cat's-paw, do you think, Ned Quinn,
To pull your poisoned chestnuts from the fire
And feed them to your foes? I told you. No.

QUINN.

You didn't think that way the day you led him
Into the room where her that's dead in there
Lay in my arms as guiltless as a baby
In a fit of drunken warmth she took for love!

JOSIE.

More shame to me I didn't think that way!
She was my own blood, and she loved the man;
And I tried to get between them, and broke her heart.
It's all my fault that she lies dead in there,
No one's but mine. And she was good to me,
And I betrayed her— Ned, she wouldn't see me.
She wouldn't let me in the room at the last.
They say she'd not confess her life with Matt;
They say she would not call that life a sin. (*Pause.*)
I'll never interfere that way again.
If it were not for me, they'd have been married,
And there'd have been no sin. Has Ag gone to Hell?
Do you think that, Ned? For that would be my fault.
Have I destroyed her life forever, Ned,
In this world and the next? (*Pause.*)

QUINN.

                              You're talking blather.
Ach, God's more merciful than Father Coyne,
Be sure of that, or we'd have been roasted black,
The whole damned lot of us, long since. (*Pause.*)
                              Come on.
Wouldn't you like to make it up to Ag, Jo?
Do something for her dead? That's all I'm asking.
Shouldn't Matt pay for what he did to her?

All that you'd need to say's a single sentence,
When the Lady Duchess Kathleen Kakiak
Descends in visitation: "Mrs. Stanton,
Sure, God will bless you for your charity."
"My charity?" she'll ask. You'll say, "You know,
Ag having lived with Matt three years and all."
That's all you'd have to say.
    JOSIE.

                          What am I, Ned,
That you take me for a fool and villain both?
Don't talk to me about your broken heart,
And how you feel you owe poor Ag revenge!
If she had wanted that, would she have died
Without the sacraments to spare Matt pain?
I know you want to drive Matt from the running
And that you'd stop at nothing short of murder
For one more term as lord of City Hall.
Best give it up, Ned. Fast. It will destroy you.
    QUINN.
Give what up, Jo?
    JOSIE.

                    Your pride. Your murderous pride.
    QUINN.
I don't know what you mean by that at all.
They're out to get me, Jo. I have to fight.
They telephoned today at half past three:
"Albany says resign or they'll destroy you!"
I had to send a letter to that bastard
Throwing in the sponge. But I'm not through yet;
And I'll win out. I always have before.
But if I go down, I won't go down alone.
You may call that pride, if you like. I call it honor.
    JOSIE.
No, Ned. Not honor, I know. Pride kept me from her.
I'd not admit the wrong was on my side,
And her with the blood of her heart on her shaking chin
In that icebox of a hallroom down in Smith Street,
The wall at her nose. Oh, Sacred Heart of Jesus,

I should have flung myself on the oilcloth floor
And not got up until she gave me pardon.
She'd have laughed at me, and called me a young whale,
Or some such nonsense. She'll never laugh again . . .
What must Matt feel?
   QUINN.

                    Good riddance to bad rubbish

Is what he feels!
   JOSIE.

               You never knew Matt, Ned,

If you think that.
   QUINN.

               I knew him well enough!—
You're still in love with him—
   JOSIE.

                  What's that to you!

   QUINN.
And him with the worst word in his mouth for you,
As he always has had!
   JOSIE.

               I don't believe you, Ned.

   QUINN.
Ah, well. Ah, well. No one believes me now.
Stanton's your god; and that's just as it should be.
You're traitors all, as fickle as the sunlight
On April Fools' Day. But there'll come a time
You'll say Ned Quinn was right.
   JOSIE.

                 What kind of thing

Is it he says of me?
   QUINN.

            No matter, now.
You'd not believe me if I told it you.
   JOSIE.
What does he say? (*Pause.*)
   QUINN,

            For one thing that you're two-faced,

And well enough, since the face that you were born with's
Like a madman's arse.
   JOSIE.

                  You son of a bitch, Ned Quinn,
That sounds like you, not him.
   QUINN.

                     Have it your own way.
I'm old, you know; I'm all dustmice upstairs.
It's hard for me to lay my mind on recollections.
Yet it seems to me I can recall a toast
Matt drank his birthday night at Villepigue's
Two weeks before we had that fight in Seagate . . .
He stood there fingering that green silk tie
That you embroidered those gold shamrocks on—
   JOSIE.
How do you know that I gave Matt that tie?
   QUINN.
He told me when he gave the tie to Petey—
   JOSIE.
You made that up! (*Pause.*)
   QUINN.

               He lifted up his glass,
And laughed, and said: "Confusion to the devil
That's bent Jo Finn as fast around my neck
As a coop around a barrel; and her legs as loose
As her lying tongue—
   JOSIE.

             God's curse on you for that!
   QUINN.
God's curse on me? I'm only telling truth.
Come to your senses, woman. He played me false.
And Ag. And her he's married to, Kathleen.
What makes you think you are the bright exception?
   JOSIE.
Because I know him for a good man, Ned.
And not a poisonous old woman of a thief,
Destroying names to keep himself in office—

QUINN.
A thief, am I! I'll get what I want without you;
And when Stanton plays you false, don't whine to me.

(*Enter* KATHLEEN, STANTON, *and* MURPHY. MURPHY *is
carrying a case of liquor, which he sets on the chair
nearest him, his eyes fixed on* QUINN *and* STANTON
confronting each other.)

STANTON.
I will not play her false, nor will I you . . .
I got your letter; and I thank you for it.
I'm sorry that my winning means your loss.

(*Pause.* QUINN *glares at* STANTON, *then takes a step towards the door.*)

MURPHY.
Wait, Ned!
   STANTON.
          I swear, I'll see you through this trouble.
I want to be your friend again. Shake hands.
Come on, man. And what better place than here.
I'm sure Ag would have wanted it. Come on—
   QUINN.
Good God! The goat can talk. When Ag was living,
   though,
You rarely met the livestock in the house!

(STANTON *hurls himself at* QUINN, *and takes him by the
throat.* KATHLEEN *screams.* JOSIE *and* MURPHY *rush
to get between them.*)

STANTON.
I'll kill him!
   MURPHY.
         Hold him back. Go on, Ned. Go.
Remember Ag, Matt. Please. No disrespect.

(MURPHY *is holding* STANTON'S *arms.* QUINN, *disengag-*

ing himself from JOSIE, *blackly looks* STANTON *up
and down, and spits in his face. It takes both* MUR-
PHY *and* KATHLEEN *to hold* STANTON *back.* QUINN
watches the struggle. Exit QUINN *slowly.* JOSIE
fetches a rag, and hands it to STANTON. *He wipes
the spittle off his face and coat.*)

JOSIE.
Pay him no heed, Matt. Sure, what need have you
To care what a thief thinks who's been found out—
   STANTON.
I'll thank you to keep out of this, Jo Finn.
You always were a one for interfering.
   JOSIE.
Why take things out on me? It was he spit at you.
   KATHLEEN.
Mattie, Mattie, are you crazed or what?
You've hurt the woman's feelings.
   STANTON.

                        Kate, come ahead.
Where are the Haggertys?
   JOSIE.

                   Inside with the rest.
Inside in the parlor.

(STANTON *takes* KATHLEEN *by the arm, but she holds
   back.*)

   KATHLEEN.
               Matt, beg her pardon.
   STANTON.
For what? For what? Don't waste your sympathy
On that one. And stay clear of her as can be:
She has a wicked tongue. Watch out for her—
   KATHLEEN.
The woman heard you!—
   STANTON.
              Devil a bit I care!
Will you come into the parlor!

KATHLEEN.

Matt, she's crying.

(STANTON *strides over towards* JOSIE, *awkward with remorse.*)

STANTON.
Josie—
    JOSIE.
        Never mind. I heard you, Matt.
    STANTON.

The devil

Take you then, for your big ears!
    JOSIE.

The devil take me, Matt.

    KATHLEEN.
Please, Mrs. Finn—
    JOSIE.

Go in now to the wake,

And let me be!

(*Pause.* MURPHY *shakes his head, and motioning* KATHLEEN *towards the portiere, holds it up for her. Exit* KATHLEEN, STANTON, *and* MURPHY. JOSIE *walks to the table and picks up the rag which* STANTON *used to wipe the spittle off himself. In a spasm of rage, she tears it in two and throws it on the floor. Enter* MARIA HAGGERTY.)

    MARIA.
What's this that Mrs. Stanton's after saying
About a fight between her man and you?
    JOSIE.
I'm not the kind that would demean myself
By having words with the likes of him, Maria.
    MARIA.
The likes of him? What is this all about?
I've never heard you talk that way of Matt.

JOSIE.
I never found him out until just now.
He treated me like dirt. And who is he
To be so high and mighty—Hogan's Goat,
A fancy boy made good! Ag's fancy boy!
MARIA.
You shut your mouth, or I will shut it for you.
Matt's broken up because of Aggie's death;
That's why he lost his temper. That and Quinn,
Bad luck be with the day I let him in here.
I'll not have you make trouble for Matt, Jo.
I want you to come into the parlor now
And take Matt's hand.
    JOSIE.

                    It's he should take my hand.
    MARIA.
Will you come in, if he comes out to you first?

(*Enter* KATHLEEN *softly behind* MARIA.)

    JOSIE.
I'll make no promises.

(*Pause.* KATHLEEN *puts her black-gloved hand on* MA-
RIA'S *shoulder.* MARIA *starts, and acknowledges her
with nervous heartiness.*)

    MARIA.
                Why, Mrs. Stanton!
    KATHLEEN.
I'd like to talk to Mrs. Finn alone. (*Pause.*)
Maria? Just a moment or two. Alone.
    (*Exit* MARIA *reluctantly.*)
Mrs. Finn, please. Matthew meant no harm . . .
He has a dreadful temper. You know that.
And he's like a scalded cat since yesterday
When he got the news that Agnes Hogan died. (*Pause.*)
He told me just how much she'd meant to him

When he was starting out on his career.
You know that better, maybe, than myself—
    JOSIE.
He told you that, did he! Did he tell you how
He lived with her three years in a state of sin
In a love nest of a roadhouse down in Seagate?
And the devil take the talk! Did he tell you, too,
She drank herself consumptive for his sake
Because he threw her over three years since,
When he'd got all he wanted from her, missis,
And married you—

(KATHLEEN *gasps and runs out the door.* JOSIE *looks
straight ahead into the air before her face, brings
both hands to her forehead with a slap, and sits
swaying in her chair.*)

CURTAIN

END OF ACT I

ACT II

SCENE 1

Eleven o'clock the same evening. The Stantons' flat. Before the Curtain rises, the sound of a SCUFFLE and a CRY. KATHLEEN stands, tight with fury, a large silver hand mirror, which she has just struck STANTON with, in her hand. STANTON sits on the edge of the couch, a handkerchief to his forehead, which is bleeding slightly. KATHLEEN turns her gaze from STANTON to the floor. With that sudden recession of energy which follows drunken violence, she sways and slumps, the hand with the mirror in it hanging slackly at her side. She kicks at the fragments of the mirror with the toe of her shoe, as if she were puzzled by them. She is very drunk, but on brandy; that is, her mind is sharper than it would seem to be.

KATHLEEN.
The mirror's broken.

STANTON.

Yes. That means bad luck.

KATHLEEN.
I know it does. But now I can see plain,
Just as it says in First Corinthians:
When I was a child, I saw as a child does,
Saw what I loved as in a mirror darkly,
But now I see his face—

STANTON.

This night of all nights!
When I have Quinn's note resigning in my hand!
The bitch of a Josie Finn with her snake's tongue!—
Where have you been till now? Where did you get it?

KATHLEEN.
Did I get what, Matt?
STANTON.

              The drink that's crazed you.

KATHLEEN.
In your own back room with a woman named Miss Legg.
Miss Bessie Legg. She'd yards and yards of beads on,
And a hat like a berry patch attacked by magpies,
And a fancy neckpiece like twelve Persian cats
All tied together. You'd think she'd blow away
At the first breeze with all those feathers on her.
STANTON.
How could you do a thing like that to me?
Get paralyzed for everyone to gawk at,
And with the district whore?
KATHLEEN.

              She's that, is she?
Birds of a feather flock together, Matt,
And whore will meet with whore. That's what I am.
We aren't married. We aren't. You know that.
Isn't it the same as you and Agnes?
STANTON.

             Jesus, Katie! (*Pause.*)

KATHLEEN.
Are you hurt bad, Matt?
STANTON.

            It's nice of you to ask.

(KATHLEEN *flies at him.*)

KATHLEEN.
You son of a bitch, I'll kill you.
    (STANTON *pinions her arms. She drops the mirror.*
    What began as battle ends as embrace.)
             Mattie, Mattie.
STANTON.
Oh, Katie, what's the matter with us both!
KATHLEEN.
What can a woman say when she learns the man

She left her country and her God to marry
Has married her to show his cast-off mistress
That he can do without her, or even worse,
Only to earn his good name back again?
   STANTON.
I married you because I love you, Kate.
   KATHLEEN.
Then why was I the one soul in this city
Who didn't know of you and Agnes? Why?
   STANTON.
I didn't want to hurt you.
   KATHLEEN.

               Well, you have—
How do I know you won't abandon me
If I don't get you what you want from life?
   STANTON.
Don't say such things.
   KATHLEEN.

            No wonder they seemed strange,
Your what-d'ya-callem's, your constituents:
They none of them could look me in the face
For fear they might let on. Didn't Bessie Legg
Tell me she thought the only reason Agnes Hogan
Went to bed with Quinn was to prove to herself
That there was someone loved her, when she saw
Your feelings for her dying like wet coal,
And realized she'd lost you? How do I know
The same thing will not happen to myself;
And people won't be saying a year from now,
Kate went the same way as the poor dead whore?
   STANTON.
Kate. Don't call her that.
   KATHLEEN.

            Why not? Don't they?
   STANTON.
They don't. And don't you call her out of name.
You never knew her. And the talk you've heard
Has been about her as she was in public,

Stripping the heavy diamonds off her fingers
To keep the party going one more hour.
I knew what lay behind it. It was mine:
Her will to fullness. She contained a man
As the wind does, the first giddy days of spring,
When your coat blows open, and your blood beats hard,
As clear as ice, and warm as a chimney wall.
'Twas she first gave me heart to dare be free.
All threats turned promise when she talked to you.
With her on your arm, you saw your life before you
Like breast-high wheat in the soft dazzle of August.
She had a way of cupping her long hands
Around my bulldog's mug, as if I were
Some fancy fruit she'd bought beyond her means,
And laughing with delight. She put nothing on
She did not feel, and felt with flesh and soul.
I don't believe she knew what shame might be.
You could not resist her. *I* could not. I tried.
I was twenty-five years old, when first I met her.
I'd never . . .

KATHLEEN.
   What?

STANTON.
     I was what you'd call a virgin . . .

KATHLEEN.
The saints preserve us!

STANTON.
     Yes, it's funny now;
It wasn't funny then. (*Pause.*)
     It was she wooed me.
It seemed—Lord knows, I don't—unnatural.
She was ten years my senior. But, oh, Kate,
To look at her downstairs, you'd never know
What once she was! Her hair was bronze and silver
Like pear trees in full bloom, her eyes were opal,
Her skin was like new milk, and her blue veins
Trembled in the shimmer of her full straight neck
Like threads of violets fallen from her hair

And filliped by the breeze. She bought me presents:
A handmade vest of black brocaded silk,
A blond Malacca cane with a silver head
Cast like an antique statue, the Lord knows what,
There were so many of them. And she'd cock
That angel's head of hers, and tell me:
"You look like such a slob, Matt, I took pity
And bought you something nice. You can pay me back . . .
Some day." (*Pause.*)
         I took them not to hurt her, Kate;
And when she asked me would I work for her,
Would I run the gaming rooms in Seagate for her,
And keep her out of trouble, I said yes;
And when she asked me would I be her man,
I'd have said yes, but I could scarcely breathe
Between the want and fear of her. I nodded—
I never knew a man say no to her
Until I did myself that Labor Day
I found her in the one bed with Ned Quinn.
I looked her in the eyes, and I said, "No!
I'll play the fancy boy to you no more." (*Pause.*)
That's what I was, Kathleen, Ag's fancy boy,
I was Hogan's Goat to everyone, Ag's stud.
All my high hopes for power and for office
Fell down around my ears like a spavined roof
When I first heard them call me that— And, Kate,
When it comes to feelings, there was my side too:
I might have been some tethered brute in the yard
The way she acted. That last year she seemed bent
On driving home to me she was all I had,
Without her, I was nothing— Even after Newark,
She never changed—

    KATHLEEN.
                What happened in Newark?—
    STANTON.

                                Nothing!
I don't know why I brought it up in the first place.
We had a fight. I left her. I went to Newark.

She followed me. We made it up. That's all.
Let's not talk about it. It brings things back.
    KATHLEEN.
You loved her, didn't you? You love her still.
    STANTON.
Ag's dead, Kathleen. How can you love a corpse?
And in my heart she's been that these three years—
Part of me lay dead as a horse in the street
In that house in Seagate, till I met you in London.
It was as if God had sent me down an angel
To bring me back from the grave. That's why I asked
    you
To marry me in that London City Hall
Without the eight weeks' wait to cry the banns,
And come back with me right away. I was afraid,
I was afraid I'd lose you, if I left
And waited here for you till the banns were cried—
I swear to you, on my dead mother's grave,
As soon as the election's past, we'll marry
Right in St. Mary's Church, and damn the gossip!
    (*Pause.*)
I didn't tell you—
    KATHLEEN.
               Why?—
    STANTON.
                      I was ashamed
That I was ever young. I wanted you
To think I knew my way around from birth.
    KATHLEEN.
Lord help us!
    STANTON.
            And somehow, even more, I was ashamed
That I had let her woo me like a girl,
And I could not resist her or say no
For three long years. It was that slavery
I was ashamed of most—

KATHLEEN.

That slavery,
My dear, is love—
STANTON.

What is it you just said?
KATHLEEN.
I'm terrible drunk.
STANTON.

Sure, don't I know that!
And if you weren't, Kate, you'd be a widow.
You'd have brained me good and proper with that mirror,
If your eye had not been blurred—
KATHLEEN.

But I see plain!
STANTON.
Come, Katie, let me help you into bed—
KATHLEEN.
You never came to look for me, did you?
STANTON.
I did. I couldn't find you.
KATHLEEN.

Tell the truth!
You were too proud. You sat up here and waited.
You knew I would come back like a hungry cat,
Like Agnes Hogan! Call to her, why don't you?
She'll stiffen in the coffin at your voice
And drag herself up those dark stairs outside
On her bare feet! They never put shoes on them.
She's back to where she was before in Ireland:
The dirt will clog her toes!
STANTON.

Oh, Jesus, Katie!
KATHLEEN.
Don't you understand me, Mattie?
STANTON.

Come on now, Kate.
The fire's sunk. You'll catch your death of cold,
If you keep up this way. Kate, come on to bed.

KATHLEEN.
No, never!
STANTON.
          Katie, Katie, what's the matter!
KATHLEEN.
I looked at her downstairs. I feel afraid.
They say death visits three before it's done.
I looked at her sewn lips, her spotted hand
With the wedding ring you never gave her on it.
They said it was her mother's. Poor Aggie, Matt!
Poor you and me!
          (*Pause.* STANTON *covers his face with his hands and
          falls to the couch.* KATHLEEN *suddenly throws her-
          self on her knees, and embraces him around the
          waist.*)
          I don't want liberty!
Don't leave me, Mattie, please. I feel afraid.

(STANTON *uncovers his face, cups the back of her head
     in his hand, and kisses her temples.*)

STANTON.
Toc-sha-shin-inish, my darling. Don't be talking—
KATHLEEN.   ·
It isn't God I want, it's you—
STANTON.
                              Sh. Sh.
KATHLEEN.
I wanted to go away, Matt; but I couldn't.
Those things you said about you and Ag Hogan,
About resenting how you felt for her,
They go for me— Oh, Matt, we're like twin children:
The pride is in our blood— I'd like to kill you,
Or die myself. Do you understand me, Matt!
Don't let me. I am sick with shame. I love you—

(STANTON *kisses her on the mouth, lifts her to her feet,
     and helps her towards the bedroom.*)

STANTON.
You're crying drunk—
  KATHLEEN.

                    In vino veritas:
There's truth in drink.
  STANTON.

                    God! Now she's quoting Latin,
And me so ignorant that all I know
Is that I'm cold and want my wife beside me
Before I can feel warm again or rest.
Ag's dead, Kate, dead.
But, Katie, we're alive.
Come with me out of the cold. Ag's gone for good.

                    CURTAIN

                    ACT II

                    SCENE 2

*Midnight the same night. The back room of Stanton's
    Saloon.* Stanton for Mayor *is spelled out in gold-
    paper letters hanging from the crepe-paper streamers.*

BESSIE LEGG *sits at a table, looking downcast and be-
    wildered, an empty glass before her, her back to the
    Ladies' Entrance. The door to the Ladies' Entrance
    swiftly opens a crack.* BILL *sticks his head in and
    withdraws it. The door swiftly closes.* BESSIE *cranes
    round, sees nothing, and returns to her glum day-
    dream. Enter* QUINN *and* BILL *through the Ladies'
    Entrance.*

  BESSIE.
Watch what the hell you're doing!
Creeping up on parties like the Blackhand!
Good Christ, it's you! What are you doing here?
You want to start a riot?

QUINN.

Go easy, Bessie,
Or you'll have them in here. I'll tell you what to do.
Go get two doubles; and tell them at the bar
You'd like to be alone in here awhile,
You have a customer.

(QUINN *puts a ten-dollar bill on the table in front of
her*.)

BESSIE.

I'm through with that.

QUINN.
I'm through with that, says she, and her stairs in splinters
From the armies charging up and down them nights!
Don't sit there that way with your mouth sprung open
Like a busted letter box. Go get the drinks.
(QUINN *moves out of sight of the bar. Exit* BESSIE,
opening and closing the door as if it were mined.)
Keep watch outside now, Bill. Give the door a kick
If you see that bastard coming. If the trunk is there,
And the box is in it, I'll pass you out the key.

(*Exit* BILL *through the Ladies' Entrance.* QUINN *walks
around the room as if examining it before taking it
over.* KICK *at the bar door.* QUINN *starts, looks towards the Ladies' Entrance, then back at the bar
door. When he sees that someone is opening the door
for* BESSIE, *he draws back into the shadows. Enter*
BESSIE *with two double whiskeys in her hand.*)

BESSIE.
When I say private, I mean private, Percy.
Didn't your mother teach you manners— Thanks for
nothing!
Pinching a person when a person's helpless!
Shut the door or you'll get a bourbon eyewash.

(*As the bar door shuts behind her, a* MALE VOICE *chants
in falsetto.*)

MALE VOICE.
Remember St. Peter's,
Remember St. Paul's,
Remember the goil
You kissed in the hall!
    BESSIE.
Honest, if there ain't more snots than noses,
I'm the Mother Superior at Good Shepherd's!
Here's your lousy drinks.
> (BESSIE *sets the doubles before herself and* QUINN
> *as she sits down. She pushes the change from the
> ten across the table.* QUINN *smiles, and pushes it
> back to her.*)

                    That was a ten-spot.
Them drinks were forty cents.

> (QUINN *smiles again, shakes his head, and motions her
> to take the money. She does, with a shamefaced
> smile. They lift their glasses to each other and
> drink.*)

    QUINN.

                    How are you since? . . .
    BESSIE.
You didn't come here for no dish of tea.
    QUINN.
As a matter of fact, I'd like to ask a favor;
And I missed you at the wake. That's why I came.
    BESSIE.
You didn't miss me, kid. I didn't go.
Dead people make me nervous. What's this favor?
    QUINN.
I hear you've been spelling out May Haggerty
Looking after Ag this past year, Bessie.
I wonder did Ag still have a cowhide trunk?
    BESSIE.
A yellow leather trunk? She did.
    QUINN.

                    Where is it?

BESSIE.
It's around the corner in her room in Smith Street,
The Haggertys didn't have time to cart it home.
    QUINN.
There's something in it that I'd like to have,
For a keepsake, don't you know. Have you the key?
    BESSIE.
The key to Ag's room? Yeah.
    QUINN.

                              Good. Give it here.

    BESSIE.
What's in this trunk you want?
    QUINN.

                              An onyx brooch.

It was my poor old mother's. I gave it Ag
When I first met her.
    BESSIE.

                    She ain't got that now.

I seen that tin box that she kept her things in
Two days ago. That's where May got the ring
They're burying Ag in. That was all there was,
That and some old papers—
    QUINN.

                              I'd like to see those too.

    BESSIE.
Why?
    QUINN.

        Why! To make sure that there are no receipts
    there
To fall into wrong hands.
    BESSIE.

                            You go ask Maisie.

I got no right to give no key to you.
Those things are hers now.
    QUINN.

                            Lord! I can't do that.

She'd go ask Matt; and then I'd never get them!

BESSIE.

I thought you wanted that thing that was your mother's.
QUINN.

I do. That onyx ring.
BESSIE.

You said a brooch.
There's something in that box that'll cause trouble.
I'm going to take and give the key to Matt.
QUINN.

I wouldn't do that, child, if I were you.
Remember what you told them in the bar,
You wanted to be alone in here awhile,
You had a customer? Shall I call the cop,
What's this his name is, Boylan's on this beat,
And have you up on lewd solicitation?
Would you like a three months' course in sewing mailbags
In the Women's Prison? Bessie, smarten up.
Hand me the key.

(BESSIE *rummages in her bag, then throws the key
and the change from the drinks on the table. She
rises, and walks towards the bar door.*)

Where do you think you're going?
BESSIE.

Ain't you finished with me yet?
QUINN.

Sit down, my dear.
You'll not leave here till the box is in my hands.
You'd be up the street and at Matt's ear in no time
Like a wasp at a pear. Sit down when I tell you to.

(BESSIE *sits down.* QUINN *opens the door to the
Ladies' Entrance. Sound of RUNNING FEET.*
QUINN *closes the door, returns to the table, and sits
down. He pushes the change from the drinks back to*
BESSIE.)

Would you like another drink while we're waiting, Bessie?—

BESSIE.

I wouldn't drink with you if I had the jimjams
And every crack in the wall had a rat's snout in it.

QUINN.

I know how my morality must offend
A fine upstanding woman like yourself—

(BESSIE *throws her whiskey in* QUINN'S *face, looks
terrified, then bursts into tears. With great coolness,*
QUINN *pulls a large silk handkerchief out of his
pocket, and blots his face and clothing.*)

You always were a great one for the crying.

BESSIE.

I guess I done some bum things in my life
But this is the first time that I ever ratted.

QUINN.

Ratted, my dear? I don't know what you mean.
I told you all I wanted was old receipts.

(*Sound of RUNNING.* BILL *runs through the Ladies' Entrance and hands* QUINN *a tin box.* QUINN
motions BILL *back out to keep watch. Exit* BILL.
QUINN *puts the box on the floor and kicks it. It
opens. He puts the box on the table.*)

I gave that box to Ag myself. The lock
Was always window dressing. For how could I know
When there might be something here I'd like to see.
Will you look at this? A bundle of scorched letters:
Matt Stanton, Esq., Care of the Gen PO,
Newark, New Jersey. That's where Mattie went
When he slipped Ag's tether in Seagate. And look, the
necktie
That Josie made for Matt, and a dried camellia,
And a pair of busted garnet rosaries.
And this, dear God in Heaven, look at this,
A letter with no salutation on it
In poor Ag's pothook script. It has no date.
"You're dead to me, because I'm dead myself.
I have been since you left me. If you think
I mean to cause you trouble for what you've done,

You never knew me. You've made your dirty bed.
Lie in it now till you feel the filth in your bones.
I—" No more. No more!—Ag always was too proud.
She never sent it.
     BESSIE.
                         Put them things all back.
They don't belong to you.
     QUINN.
                              Wait now. Wait now.
There's a trick to this false bottom. There it goes.
If it's not the kind of receipt I knew would be here!
It's charred. She meant to burn it. But you can read it.
     BESSIE.
Give me them things.
     QUINN.
                         I only want this, Bessie.
     (QUINN *puts the paper in his pocket.*)
I'm through now. We can part. Don't worry, child.
I'm putting these things in the box, and Bill will return it
And lock the trunk and room behind him. But mark me.
You're not to say a thing of this to Stanton.
He's a worse suspicious nature than your own;
And we've got to come, you know, to a meeting of minds
At the Clambake on my birthday Sunday, Bessie,
Stanton and I. It would only throw him off
If he heard I had been going through Ag's things.
We wouldn't want that, Bessie; would we, child,
Any more than you'd want that stretch in jail.
I hope you take my meaning— I must leave you, Bessie.

(QUINN *rises with the box under his arm, and moves to-
     wards the Ladies' Entrance.*)

     BESSIE.
I hope you rot in Hell!
     QUINN.
                         You must love me, child,
That you should want my company forever.

(*Exit* QUINN. *Sound of a HACK rolling off.* BESSIE *grabs the money off the table and crumples it up in her hands. She looks at the door and at the money. She puts the money in her bag and bursts out crying.*)

CURTAIN

ACT II

SCENE 3

Twilight, the evening of Sunday, May 1, 1890. The stern of a Coney Island steamer bound for Seagate. The lower deck is overhung with an upper, upon which people pass from time to time. There are two oval portraits, one of STANTON, *the other of* QUINN, *suspended from the railings of the upper deck, above entrances to Stage Right and Stage Left. Between them, there is a large shield printed in bold Pontiac reading* For the Public Good. *The shield and portraits are hung over swagged bunting. On the lower deck, to Stage Right, there is a table with a cluster of carpet-seated folding chairs around it. Set off a little from them, its back to the table, there is a carpet-seated armchair.*

HAGGERTY, BOYLE, *and* ANN MULCAHY *are seated at the table.* HAGGERTY *is wearing a green-and-gold sash with* The Matthew Stanton Association *printed on it. Enter* MARIA HAGGERTY *with a large, loaded tea tray, which she sets on the table. She pours and passes the tea.*

MARIA.
One hour more. and we'll be into Seagate.
That's what the deckhand says. I'm glad of that.
Two hours more of sailing, I declare to God,
And the babies all would be drunk in their carriages.

HAGGERTY.

Where's missis, May? Will I bring her tea to her?

MARIA.

No. Let her sleep. She's dozed off in Matt's stateroom.
The brandy must have killed the queasiness.

ANN.

Wasn't that a grand speech Ned Quinn made
Before Matt came, on the pier at Fulton Street,
When he said he was glad he'd arranged the Clambake
    late,
So that he could begin his voyage into the evening,
His loyal supporters at his side to the end.

BOYLE.

I'm coming. I'm coming.
And my belly's full of gin.
I hear their drunken voices calling
Old Ned Quinn.

HAGGERTY.

Don't dance on Quinn's grave, Petey. It's unlucky.
We're not through this night yet.

MARIA.

                              True for you there, Jack!
They've yet to make the bad blood up between them.
Father Coyne's been in Quinn's stateroom this past hour,
And Palsy's been at Matt in the Saloon Bar.
Quinn wants Mattie to come to *him;* and Matt
Won't move an inch towards him till Quinn begs his par
    don
For spitting in his face at Aggie's wake.

HAGGERTY.

Woman, shut up. No call to worry that much.
If you knew politics as well as I do,
You'd see they'll both bow down to a higher law
Before this night is out.

BOYLE.

                    St. Albany,
Pray for us.

HAGGERTY.
            Stop your blaspheming, Petey.
I don't mean Albany, but the public good—

(*Enter* BESSIE LEGG, *Stage Right, in a rush.*)

BESSIE.
Oh, Petey. Petey. Come to the front of the boat.
You can see the electra light from Coney there,
And that hotel they built like a elephant.
Why don't youse all come. God, it's beautiful.

(*Exit* BOYLE *and* BESSIE, *the* HAGGERTYS *and* ANN, *Stage Right.*)

BOYLE.
I asked me mother for fifty cents,
To see the elephant jump the fence.
He jumped so high, he touched the sky,
And never come down till the Fourt' of July.

The Fourt' of July when he crashed to earth
He landed near my fat Aunt Gert.
She says you lumpy pig-eyed skunk
Stay off that sauce if you get that drunk.

(*Sound of their LAUGHTER fading. Enter* QUINN *and* BILL, *with* FATHER COYNE *following, Stage Left.*)

FATHER COYNE.
You'll meet with him here then?
    QUINN.
                        Yes, Father, I will.
I'll meet with him anywhere. But he'll come to me.
    FATHER COYNE.
I'll go and get him.

(*Exit* FATHER COYNE, *Stage Left.* QUINN *stands back and looks at the shield and posters.*)

QUINN.
> Look at that now, Billy.
Brooklyn, how are you! For the public good!
A whore for a mayor and a spoiled nun for his lady!
We mustn't let that happen, must we now?—
Play lose me, Billy. Here's the lot of them.
> (*Exit* BILL, *Stage Right. Enter* FATHER COYNE, *followed by* MURPHY *and* STANTON. STANTON *walks forward, keeping his eyes straight ahead.* QUINN *rakes all three of them with his eyes, then averts his gaze from* STANTON. QUINN, *to* MURPHY.)
If it isn't the Lord Beaconsfield of Brooklyn
With the ten thumbs of his fine Italian hands
Done up in ice-cream gloves.
> (*He turns suddenly to* STANTON.)
> How are you since?—

STANTON.
I'll speak no word until he begs my pardon.
I told you, Father. Has he grown so old and silly
He thinks men can do harm without amends!

FATHER COYNE.
Do you want him to get down on his knees to you!
He's lost enough already. Leave him his pride.

MURPHY.
The food in the mouth of the voters is at stake,
It's bread and lard for lunch for thousands, thousands,
If this election's lost; and it will be lost
Unless you join your hands and pull together.

QUINN.
For all that's passed between us, I'll shake his hand,
If he will mine.

MURPHY.
> Come on now, Matt. Come on.

QUINN.
When he gets as old as I am, he'll understand
It was death I spat at that night at the wake,
And wish he'd come to terms with an old man's rage.

(*Pause.* STANTON *suddenly grabs* QUINN's *hand.* QUINN
    gives him a clumsy bear hug, his face appearing over
    STANTON's *shoulder.*)

STANTON.
Go on now, Ned. You're not that old. You've years.
There's years of use in you.
    QUINN.
                    Matt boy.

MURPHY.
They say that when a man shakes hands with his foe,
A suffering soul shoots out of Purgatory
Straight into Heaven, like a lark from a cage.
    FATHER COYNE.
What Council was it, Palsy, declared that dogma?
    QUINN.
Sister Mary Asafoetida Doyle,
His fourth-grade teacher.
    MURPHY.
                    To the Saloon Bar!
Drinks for all comers, and on the Party too!

(MURPHY *and* FATHER COYNE *move towards the exit,*
    Stage Left, with QUINN *and* STANTON *a few paces*
    behind them.)

QUINN.
You know, Matt, if you left the landing to me,
I could drive it home to all what terms we're on,
And make the kind of an occasion of it
Your missis would remember all her life.
With both the bands of our Associations
Thundering and ringing out below us
And all the voters stamping and applauding,
I'd like to take your wife and you by the hand
And bring you down. A little taste of glory
Has never done a creature any harm—
    STANTON.
That's just the thing, maybe, might pick her up.

The water made her qualmish and she lay down—
You've never met Kathleen to talk to, have you?
Come down with me now, and I will introduce you.

(*Exit* FATHER COYNE *and* MURPHY, QUINN *and* STAN-
TON, *Stage Left. Pause. Enter* KATHLEEN *slowly,
Stage Right. She is dressed in a black traveling suit
and is wearing a large black hat. She stands looking
at the wake of the steamer a moment, moves the
armchair into the shadows, and sits in it, her back
to the soft bustle of* VOICES *coming towards her.
Pause. Enter the* HAGGERTYS, ANN MULCAHY,
BOYLE, *and* BESSIE. *They do not notice* KATHLEEN.
MARIA *is carrying yet another large pot of tea, and
herding* HAGGERTY *before her.*)

HAGGERTY.
You'll have my kidneys burst with all that tea.
   MARIA.
Never mind. You've a night of drink before you.
Keep moving, bullhead.
   HAGGERTY.
                    Have a little respect.
   BESSIE.
Didn't I tell youse it was beautiful!
   ANN.
Going back to Seagate's a bit sad
With poor Ag in the ground just yesterday.
   BESSIE.
Yeah. Ain't it. Yeah. I wish it was Coney instead.
The shoot-the-chutes—
   BOYLE.
                    The tunnel of love.
   BESSIE.
                                   Oh, Petey.
   ANN.
Will you ever forget the Clambake Aggie gave us
Three years ago, on that lovely stretch of beach!

We'd pails of clams and oysters, steamed and fresh,
And pounds of butter in round wooden tubs,
And crabs and lobsters bigger than our heads,
Chickens and potatoes, roasted corn—
    BOYLE.
And wagonloads of beer.
    HAGGERTY.

                And good beer too.

    ANN.
And all day long the men with accordeens
Went weaving in and out us on the sand
Till the stars were thick and near us in the sky.
    MARIA.
And Aggie, God have mercy on her soul,
Got skittish when they freshened up the fires,
And danced a jig on three kegs roped together,
With all them little bells she used to sew
Into the hems of her dresses ringing thin
Like birds at dawn. (*Pause.*)
    HAGGERTY.

              She nearly broke her arse.

    MARIA.
John Haggerty!
    HAGGERTY.

            She did! Don't look at me so stark.
One keghead gave, and she went on her ear.
She showed us everything she had that time,
The clocks of her stockings to her knicker buttons,
Acres and acres of somersaulting drawers.
Amn't I right, Pete boy?
    BOYLE.

             You're right as rain.

    BESSIE.
You was too young to notice.

(BOYLE *pulls the lower eyelid of his left eye down with
    his left forefinger.*)

BOYLE.

Do you see green?—
That was the night Matt found Ag playing tigress
To Tiger Quinn.

MARIA.

You shut your mouth, Pete Boyle.

BOYLE.

He said she broke her ass!

HAGGERTY.

That wasn't gossip.
It was a simple statement of pure fact,
To use the lawyer's parlance.

MARIA.

The lawyers' parlance!
Drink your tea, you omadhaun. You're drunk.
Shut up and drink your tea.

HAGGERTY.

"Ah, man! Proud man!
Dressed in a little brief authority"—

(MARIA *gives him what she'd call "one look."*)
I'm drinking it fast as I can! My mouth's destroyed!

BESSIE.

You should see Pete jigging. He's the best there is.
He learned me how.

BOYLE.

Get up and we'll show them, kid.

HAGGERTY.

They'll show us, will they! Stand up to me there, woman,
And show them how we won the branch and bottle
On the pounded clay of every Kerry crossroads.

(MARIA *and* HAGGERTY *begin the jig with* BOYLE *and*
BESSIE *doing a little shuffle all their own.* ANN *remains seated, helpless with shamefaced laughter.*
KATHLEEN *rises and, standing half in the shadows,
watches them with a shy smile. They are too en-
grossed to notice her.*)

BOYLE.
He gave it to Maisie;
It near drove her crazy,
The leg of the duck!
The leg of the duck!
> (*Enter* STANTON, *searching for* KATHLEEN. *He looks amused; but when he sees* KATHLEEN, *his face blackens.*)

I gave it to Bessie;
She says it was messy,
The leg of the duck!
The leg of the duck!
STANTON.
What kind of song is that in front of my wife?
HAGGERTY.
We didn't see her, Matt.
STANTON.
                                        Are you blind or what!
You, you narrow-back plug, with your mouth of slime,
You can slather this one all that you've a mind to,
But there are others born with a little shame!—
I'd be amazed at you two, May and Jack,
If I'd not noticed the liberties you've been taking
These past few months. There'll be an end to that.
HAGGERTY.
All right. All right. There'll be an end to that . . .
Come, May and Ann, we'd best go inside now.
BOYLE.
Wait; we'll come too. I'll lug these things for you.

> (*All* FOUR *move towards the exit to Stage Right.*)

KATHLEEN.
Maria, dear, come back in a few minutes.
I need you. Please. I'm not myself at all.
MARIA.
Yes, ma'am. Yes, ma'am.

> (*Exit* BOYLE *and* BESSIE, HAGGERTY *and* MARIA.)

KATHLEEN.

                     Beg their pardon, Mattie.
They didn't see me; and what harm if they did,
They were only dancing.

STANTON.

                   Things have changed now, Kate.
You have to demand respect, or you won't get it.
From this day on, they're to learn their place and keep it.
We're with them, but not of them.—Kate, I've won!
Quinn and I made it up and he wants to meet you.

KATHLEEN.

If that's what winning means, God help us both.

STANTON.

What's the matter with you?

KATHLEEN.

                   It's being aboard a ship,
It's that, I suppose. When I watch the wake of the boat
Spread out like a pigeon's tail with the wind going
    through it,
I think of all that's left behind or canceled,
And the heart of me feels pillaged in my breast.
The farther away I go from what is past,
The more I stiffen with the sense of danger.
I look around me at all, and want to hold it:
May dancing there with her back straight as a bowstring
Despite the tug of age on all her bones,
And the dazzle of Jack's eyes as they browsed her face,
And Ann Mulcahy helpless with pure joy,
And that dusty weed of a boy and Bessie Legg,
Playing their little games like aging children.
There's not a thing that is not riches, Mattie,
And it all goes from us, darling, like those days
On the boat from England, glazed with salt and sunshine,
We melted first into light like flame and candle,
It all goes from us. Hold me, Mattie, hold me.
Don't thrust me from you as you just did them.

STANTON.

Katie, I'd sooner hack the hands from my wrists

Than thrust you from me. As for what's been lost,
God in Heaven be with the days I lay
Like a bee in a lily with the ocean's glitter
Live gold on the stateroom panels. They were good.
But what's ahead, you'll not believe till you see it.
We've won! We've won, Kate! Quinn's arranged our
    landing:
You'll be breathing music like the saints in Heaven
As you walk ashore. But let him tell it you.
      (STANTON *kisses her.*)
What is that? Brandy, that I smell on you?
    KATHLEEN.
I took a glass or two for the seasickness.
    STANTON.
Promise me on your dead parents' grave,
You'll drink no more from this time forward, Kate.
There's no sight worse on earth than a drunken woman.
I know it to my shame, from her that's dead. (*Pause.*)
    KATHLEEN.
. . . I promise, Mattie.

      (STANTON *kisses her hand.*)

STANTON.
              There now. I'll get the mayor.

(*Exit* STANTON, *Stage Left.* BESSIE *emerges from the
    shadows, Stage Right, and hurries over to* KATH-
    LEEN.)

    BESSIE.
You mind if I sit down? Remember me?
    KATHLEEN.
Of course, I do, Miss Legg. Please do sit down.
I'm pleased to see you.
    BESSIE.
              It isn't Miss. It's Mrs.
    KATHLEEN.
Yes. Mrs. Legg. Of course.

BESSIE.

                                    Was he that mad
Just for that dirty song that Petey sung,
Or was it something that Quinn said to him
That he took out on us? You know what I mean.
    KATHLEEN.
No, I don't, Miss Legg. I don't know what you mean.
    BESSIE.
Not Miss. It's Mrs.
    KATHLEEN.

                            What would the mayor say?
Matt's just gone in to get him. They're friends now.
    BESSIE.
They're friends now. Yeah. They're friends.
    KATHLEEN.

                                    What is it, please?
    BESSIE.
Oh, he hurted my feelings, see, the way he talked,
And I got nervous. I'm a nervous girl.
That, and you know, what you said up my flat that night,
About there was some mix-up in the marriage.
It sounded so romantic when you said it,
"The man I left my God and country to marry."
I couldn't make it out. You was awful . . . you know.
    KATHLEEN.
If I said that, I was awful drunk indeed.
You didn't believe me, did you, Mrs. Legg?
    BESSIE.
Oh, no. Oh, no. But I don't know where you was
Before I went and took you up my flat.
I thought that maybe Quinn got wind of it——
    KATHLEEN.
I hope you've not repeated what I said.
You haven't, have you?

                    (BESSIE *rises*.)

    BESSIE.

                            Excuse me. I'll be going.

KATHLEEN.
Now don't be that way.
   BESSIE.

                  What do you think I am,
Some kind of rat . . . I thought you was a sport.
You're like the rest . . . Oh, I seen you looking round
When I brought you back up my flat that night.
It's not my fault the place is such a mess.
I only rent it, see? It isn't mine.
And we only just got in when you passed out—
I mean, fell off to sleep . . . I didn't like
To make no noise . . . It's hard to keep things nice.
There was a time I had things beautiful.
When Legg was living with me, Legg, you know,
My husband . . . I passed the flat we used to have
On Baltic Street and Court the other day.
We lived in it two years. I kept it spotless . . .
The windows all were dirty when I passed,
The windows of the flat we used to have,
I mean. All dirty . . . It nearly broke my heart.
I had a lovely home. I used to have . . .
Canary bird. Piano. Everything—
It's not my fault Legg left. Where he is, Christ knows.
Maybe he's dead. I hope to God he is,
May God forgive me, but I hope he is!

(BESSIE *bursts into tears.* KATHLEEN *rises and comforts
    her. Enter* BOYLE, *Stage Right.*)

   KATHLEEN.
Oh, Bessie, Bessie, God in Heaven help us.
   BOYLE.
Who turned on the hydrants?
   BESSIE.

                    Hello, Petey.
Buy me a drink or something, will you, ha?
   BOYLE.
Sure, kid, sure.

(BOYLE *walks to the exit, Stage Right.* KATHLEEN *and*
    BESSIE *look at one another.*)

KATHLEEN.

Goodbye.

BOYLE.

You coming, Little Eva?

(*Exit* BOYLE. BESSIE *walks to the exit, then turns to*
    KATHLEEN *again.*)

BESSIE.

Don't worry, missis. Don't. There ain't no call.
There ain't no one can hurt you. You're a lady.

(*Exit* BESSIE. KATHLEEN *walks to the rail and looks at*
    the wake of the steamer. Sound of a SHIP'S BELL.
    Enter MARIA *with a water glass of brandy.*)

DECKHAND.

Seagate. Seagate. In ten minutes. Seagate.

MARIA.

I brought you this.

KATHLEEN.

I won't. I promised Matt—

MARIA.

House devil and street saint, sure, he's worse than Quinn!
He's down there now with Quinn playing king of England.
He traipses up to me in the Saloon Bar
And takes my hand and thrusts ten dollars in it.
He's not dead yet! There'll come a time he'll see
There are some things in the world you can't take back.
If I could get a job, we'd move. We would—

(KATHLEEN *presses her fist to her mouth and sinks*
    into the armchair.)

Good Jesus, Mrs. Stanton, what's the matter!
Promise or no, best have a drop of this.

(KATHLEEN *downs half the glass of brandy.*)

KATHLEEN.
Promise or no.
MARIA.
                You'll feel the good of that.

(Pause. Sound of SHIP'S BELL and of the PADDLE churning water for the turn inshore.)

KATHLEEN.
Do you know what I am thinking about, Maria?
How it is this time of year back home in Ireland.
The foxglove has come out in the boreens,
And the seals are barking on the mossy rocks
Below Mount Brandon. On this very day,
They'll dress the loveliest girl in all the village
In a wedding gown, and lead her to the church
To put a crown of roses on the Virgin.
And all the children in Communion clothes,
White suits and dresses, smilax wreaths, pearl prayer
    books,
Will stand around her as she climbs the ladder,
And sing that song that always makes me cry:
Daughter of a mighty Father,
Maiden, patron of the May,
Angel forms around thee gather,
Macula non est in te.
Macula non est in te: Never spot was found in thee.

(KATHLEEN *breaks into tears.*)

MARIA.
Oh, Mrs. Stanton.
KATHLEEN.
                What's the matter with me?
My ears are ringing like a field of weeds,
Noontime in August, when the sun's raw fire.
MARIA.
I wonder is it flashes.

KATHLEEN.

At my age!

MARIA.

More likely kicks. Are you all together, missis.

KATHLEEN.

Am I what, Maria?

MARIA.

Have you missed your term?
Don't bite your lip and blush. You're not a nun.

KATHLEEN.

No, I've not missed my term.

(*Enter* QUINN, *Stage Left. He stands looking over at*
  MARIA *and* KATHLEEN, *unnoticed by them at first.*)

MARIA.

Then it's the dead.

KATHLEEN.

The dead?

MARIA.

The dead. Who do you know needs prayers?
They say that's how the dead call on the living,
By whining in their blood.

KATHLEEN.

Poor Agnes Hogan,
The Lord have mercy on her and preserve her . . .
    (KATHLEEN *notices* QUINN.)
Don't look so troubled, May. I'm better now.
You know there's a bottle of that Worth perfume
Down in the stateroom in my reticule.
Would you bring it to me, dear, with a handkerchief.

(*Exit* MARIA, *Stage Right.* QUINN *walks over to* KATH-
  LEEN.)

QUINN.

Good evening to you, Mrs. Stanton. May I?

KATHLEEN.

Please do, Your Honor.

(QUINN *sits down.*)

QUINN.

                Matt's stuck in the bar,
Buying drinks for all the upright voters,
So I came up alone. It would fill your eye
To see him there. You'd think he trusted them!

KATHLEEN.
God forbid he shouldn't trust them, Mayor.

QUINN.
If you think, my dear, not trusting people's a sin,
You'd best get out of politics.

KATHLEEN.
                    It's the worst sin.
Without trust, there's no faith or hope or love.

QUINN.
That kind of talk is like a penny cream puff,
All wind and whey, and deadly when it sours.
Trust no one. No one. Let no man too close.
They are as quick to fury as to love.
Once give them purchase, they will pull you down,
And for a sigh let slip, for a ruptured smile.
They're a pack of wicked mutts that go for shadows.
There is no reason in their ugliness,
No justice in their rage. Trust no one, missis.

KATHLEEN.
Who are "they"? Is it my husband, Mayor,
Or old John Haggerty or Mister Murphy?
From what you say, you think the people devils
Who've honored you as mayor of this city
For thirty years. Do you really think them that?

QUINN.
I do . . . And Stanton is the worst of all!—

KATHLEEN.
Do you think I'll sit and listen to your slander!

QUINN.
"Do you think this? Do you think this?" Or "Don't
you?"

"Faith and hope and love," and I mustn't slander—
You're awful pious for a woman living
With your husband in a state of Mortal Sin;
And a Mortal Sin it is for a Catholic woman
To marry a man outside the Catholic Church.
I don't know much religion, but I know that,
As, I might add, do all our holy voters. (*Pause.*)
    KATHLEEN.

I suppose you must have got that from Miss Legg.
    QUINN.

No, my dear. From England. Where you did it.
I've known it years. I hoped I'd not have to use it,
But need is need. And it's not Miss. It's Mrs.
    KATHLEEN.

You rejoice when people go wrong, don't you, Mayor!
    QUINN.

We've no time now to talk morality.
We'll wait for Stanton, then go get Father Coyne
And the rest, and walk down to my stateroom
And arrange what we will say. I've bought off those ac-
    countants,
Paid back that little sum from the funds I borrowed,
And the books are doctored. All that now remains is
To find a way to break the joyous news
That I will run again. I think Matt should do it!
    KATHLEEN.

If you're a man who'd ruin two reputations
To gain your ends, what have you done with your life?
    QUINN.

What I have done with my life is my affair!
Do you think I'll let that bastard have my office?
I loved the woman that he took from me,
And I let her go with him, but I kept my office.
And I heard them here in Seagate making sport
Of all I'd done for them, but I kept mum,
And I kept my office. And I watched the poor bitch die
While he grew high and mighty, but I kept my office.

Keep my office I will to the day I die,
And God help those who try to take it.
   KATHLEEN.
                                    Make sense.
The scandal about the funds is a public fact;
But you and Mrs. Legg are the only ones
Who know about the marriage. Spare my husband.
Spare him, Mayor. God will bless you for it.
   QUINN.
Sure, that's what Aggie said when she pleaded for him,
The first time that she met him, the poor slob,
Did God bless her, missis?
   KATHLEEN.
                        They'll never let you run!
They'll gang up with the Party of Reform
And crucify you.
   QUINN.
               We'll see about that, missis.
Do you think I'll let them turn their backs on me
And turn their backs on me for the likes of him,
A narrow-back pimp, who rose to where he is
On the broken heart of the woman that I loved!
   KATHLEEN.
Pour all the venom you want into my ears!
The Party will stand by us! They'll stand by us.
They'll cover us on the marriage. And they should!
For though we were not married in the Church,
May God forgive us, we are man and wife! (*Pause.*)
   QUINN.
I wouldn't be too sure of that now, missis.
   KATHLEEN.
What do you mean by that, you lying devil?

(QUINN *pulls a scorched paper out of his pocket, and
    throws it into* KATHLEEN'S *lap.*)

   QUINN.
I'm a lying devil, am I! Look at that!

Look at it, why don't you. Are you blind!
How can you be his wife when he married Ag
In the Sacred Heart in Newark in '86!

(*Repeated sound of SHIP'S BELL. People are gathering,
preparing to get off. Sound of winches, lowering
gangplank. KATHLEEN sits as if shot, the paper in
her hands.*)

DECKHAND.
Seagate! Seagate! Everybody off.
     KATHLEEN.
All gone. All gone.
     (KATHLEEN *rises suddenly, the paper in her hand,
swaying with shock, as if drunk. The disembarking
passengers look curiously at her.*)
                    God damn the day I met him.
God damn this mouth that spoke him fair, these eyes
That flooded my blood with his face. God damn this flesh
That kindled in his arms, and this heart that told me,
Say yes, say yes, to everything he asked.
It would have been better had I not been born.

(QUINN *grabs the paper out of* KATHLEEN'S *hand and
puts it back into his pocket fast.*)

     QUINN.
For God's sake, missis. Don't take on this way.
We have to keep this quiet. There's people watching.

(QUINN *runs to the table and fetches the half-finished
glass of brandy.* KATHLEEN, *still swaying, her arms at
her side, automatically accepts the glass from him
and, as if by reflex, presses it to her breast. She
does not see the people who are staring at her. Enter* STANTON *with* MURPHY *and* FATHER COYNE, *a
group of voters around him.*)

STANTON.
It isn't in the courts reform must work
But in each striving heart . . .
> (STANTON *sees the people staring at* KATHLEEN *and*
> QUINN. *He breaks away from those around him and*
> *hurries over to her. He speaks in a steely whisper.*)

Look at you. Look at you, for the love of Jesus.
In front of all these people. You're owl-eyed drunk,
With the bands about to fife us off the boat!
I'll get Maria to help you sober up.
Quinn and I will walk ashore together.
You are not fit for decent men to be seen with!

(KATHLEEN *smashes the glass to the floor. She speaks in*
a ringing voice.)

KATHLEEN.
Did you think that—
Did you think that when you lied to me in London,
And I let you marry me in the City Hall,
Because you said you couldn't wait for the banns,
You wanted me so much! Did you think that
When you had me in the bed in sacrilege
Above the corpse of your true-wedded wife,
Ag Hogan!

(*Hostile reaction from the* CROWD. *The sound of the*
BANDS suddenly blares out.)

CURTAIN

ACT II

SCENE 4

Very late the same night. The double set. There is a dim
light in the hall by the Haggertys' door; and the light
in Stanton's flat is on full. There are two trunks in

the parlor, one already locked, the other open. KATH-
LEEN *moves in and out of the bedroom, packing.*
Enter FATHER COYNE *and* MURPHY, *the* HAGGER-
TYS, BOYLE, *and* BESSIE. *The* HAGGERTYS *and* BOYLE
*are laden down with baskets and pillows done up in
steamer blankets, and have the tired, apprehensive
look of new immigrants.* HAGGERTY *sets down his
basket and unlocks the door.*

MARIA.
Open it, can't you! He may be right behind us.
And I'll not stand in the one hall with him!—
We'll be out of here before the week is done,
If I have to beg to do it—
　　FATHER COYNE.
　　　　　　　　　　　　Now, Maria—
　　MARIA.
Now Maria, Father? Are we saints!
If he got on his knees to me, I'd not forgive him!
　　MURPHY.
It's grand of you to let us wait here for him.
You must be tired.

(HAGGERTY *opens the door.*)

MARIA.
　　　　　　　　　I'll not close an eye
Until I'm out from underneath this roof!
　　HAGGERTY.
Come in the parlor, Father. I'll light the fire.
You're famished with the cold. May, bring the whiskey.
Come in now, Pete. Come in all.

(MARIA, FATHER COYNE, MURPHY, BOYLE, *and* BESSIE
pass through the portiere, followed by HAGGERTY.
Pause. KATHLEEN *moves in and out of the parlor,
packing. Enter* STANTON. *He runs lightly up the stairs
and into the parlor. He looks at the trunks and falls*

into a chair. Enter KATHLEEN, *with some clothes.*
She sees him, averts her gaze, and puts the clothes
into the trunk.)

STANTON.
Where do you think you're going!
  (KATHLEEN *passes back into the bedroom for more*
  clothes and returns with them.)
          Answer me!

KATHLEEN.
I'm going home.
  STANTON.
      Your home is here with me.

KATHLEEN.
You haven't even the grace to beg my pardon!
How can you look me in the face again!
  STANTON.
It's I should ask that question. It's all over.
They gave the nomination back to Quinn.
He brought me to the pitch of hope and betrayed me.
And you stood by and let him do it to me!
  KATHLEEN.
It ill becomes you, man, to talk betrayals.
Can you tell me whom you've known you've not be-
  trayed!—
You killed Ag Hogan. But you won't kill me!
  STANTON.
I had the right to leave her. She played me false—
  KATHLEEN.
Had you the right to marry me? The right
To cut me off from all that I hold holy?
  STANTON.
Would "all that you hold holy," our precious Church,
Have granted me a divorce from Agnes Hogan,
An adulteress!—
  KATHLEEN.
      What kind of man are you!
That woman died without the Sacraments

Because in her last fever she was afraid
If she confessed her sins she might betray you.
She died cut off from God to spare you harm.
And you have the worst word in your mouth for her.
Do you know why? Because you're no good, man.
You waited for your chance to throw her over.
You saw that with her you'd be nothing. Nothing.
You had to be the mayor of this city
And she was in the way. You married me
To make yourself respectable again.
That's the only reason.

   STANTON.

               I loved . . . I loved you, Kate.
Kathleen, I've nothing left.
I need you.

   KATHLEEN.

          Yes. To patch your kick-down fences.
But I have my pride too!—

   STANTON.

          Go then, God damn you!
Do you think I'll kneel on the floor and beg your help!
I never begged for help from man or God,
And I won't now. You'll not drive me to my knees!

   KATHLEEN.
To sit and tell me you have nothing left!
No more do I! You've taken it out of me
By demanding more than anyone can give.
That's what evil is,
The starvation of a heart with nothing in it
To make the world around it nothing too.
You never begged from man or God! You took!
You've taken all your life without return!
You never gave yourself to a single soul
For all your noble talk.—Even in bed
You stole me blind!—

   STANTON.

         Get out of here! Get out!

You're not a woman. You're a would-be nun!
You were from the beginning.
> KATHLEEN.
>> God help you, Matt.
>> (KATHLEEN *closes and locks the second trunk, and
>> puts on her hat.*)

I'll book my passage quickly as I can.
There's nothing in those trunks your money bought me.
Leave May the key. The Express will call for them.
I put the jewelry in the velvet box
In the top drawer of the bureau by the window;
And left the dresses and the sable coat
Hanging in your wardrobe. And that perfume
You bought me's on the vanity.
> (KATHLEEN *walks out the door to the head of the
> stairs.*)
>> Don't look so black.

You're free now, Matt. That's what you always wanted.
Marry if you like.
> (KATHLEEN *almost breaks down.*)
>> I'm not your wife. I never was.
> STANTON.

You mean to leave me here alone!
> KATHLEEN.
>> I'm sorry, man;

But that's the way we all are, but for God.
> (STANTON *rushes out the door and grabs* KATH-
> LEEN.)
> STANTON.

You'll not leave me! I'll see to that!

> (*BLACKOUT.* KATHLEEN *screams and hits the bottom
> of the stairs.* MARIA *rushes into the kitchen with a
> kerosene lamp in her hand, followed by* HAGGERTY,
> FATHER COYNE, MURPHY, BOYLE, *and* BESSIE.
> BOYLE *is carrying a glass of whiskey.* HAGGERTY
> flings open the door, revealing* KATHLEEN *at the

foot of the stairs in a heap, and STANTON *halfway
down the flight in a near faint.*)

HAGGERTY.
Good Jesus, May! How did it happen, man?
Give me your whiskey, Pete. Poor Mrs. Stanton.
    KATHLEEN.
Ah, Jack. And May. And is that the Father there?
Amn't I a shame and a disgrace
To get so legless drunk I fall downstairs
Like an unwatched child—
    STANTON.

                       Oh, Katie. Katie, Katie.
Are you hurt bad.
    KATHLEEN.

            Sh!
    HAGGERTY.

                     Petey, go get Boylan on the beat,
And tell him to get a doctor that's still up,
There's been an accident—
    KATHLEEN.

                  That's right. That's right.
I caught my heel on the baluster and fell.
    BOYLE.
I seen a man fall off a hoist through a hold
On Pier Sixteen down in the Erie Basin.
His head was bent that way. Her neck is broke—
    HAGGERTY.
Don't stand there nattering. Go get the doctor.

(*Exit* BOYLE, *running.*)

    MURPHY.
I'd best go too. I've a thing to do, I must.

(STANTON *takes* KATHLEEN *from* HAGGERTY *and cradles
her in his arms.*)

    STANTON.
Will you get away from her so I can hold her!

HAGGERTY.
Be careful with her—
   STANTON.
                      Katie, you were right.
I've taken without returning all my life.
And I'd the face to call Ned Quinn corrupt!
The harm I've done and called it good! The harm!
I saw that harm in Aggie Hogan's face,
And now I see it in yours. Can you forgive me?
   KATHLEEN.
Hush now, Matt darling. Toc-sha-shin-inish:
Let others talk. We'll keep our own safe counsel.
There's been shame enough already without more—
Do you know what stopped my breath up on the landing?
I love you still. I thought of us on the boat from England.
There's few have been as happy as we were—
Is that the Father there? I want the Father.

(*Enter* BOYLE *with the* POLICEMAN, BOYLAN, *and a* DOC-
    TOR.)

   FATHER COYNE.
Here I am, child. Here I am right beside you.

(FATHER COYNE *leans over* KATHLEEN, *putting on his*
    stole as he does so.)

   KATHLEEN.
Oh . . . my God . . . I am . . . heartily sorry
For . . . having . . . offended Thee—

(STANTON *pulls* KATHLEEN *away from the priest in a*
    tight embrace.)

   STANTON.
You're not to die!
   KATHLEEN.
              The boat from England, Mattie . . .

(STANTON *kisses her on the mouth, and hugs her to him,*
    his hand on the back of her head.)

STANTON.
Yes, we'll have that again. I'll make it up to you.
I'll make it up. We'll go back home to Ireland.
I'll give The Court Café to Jack to run,
And we'll go home, and take a high-stooped house
In one of them good squares, I mean, those squares . . .
        (STANTON *loosens his embrace to look in* KATH-
        LEEN'S *face. Her head falls to the side.*)
Why don't you answer me? Don't turn away!—
Where in the name of Jesus Christ's the doctor?

(*The* DOCTOR *kneels and puts his ear to* KATHLEEN'S
    *chest. He rises with a negative shudder of his head
    to* HAGGERTY. FATHER COYNE *motions* BOYLAN *and
    the* DOCTOR *out with his head. Exit* BOTH. *Pause.*)

HAGGERTY.
She's dead, you know, Matt boy.
    STANTON.
                            You're lying, man!
Do you think I have no feeling in my flesh!
She's warm as a newborn child. We're going home—
        (STANTON *loosens his embrace again.* KATHLEEN'S
        hair comes down.)
I've sprung her hairpins on her—God in heaven,
I was making love to nothing. She is dead.
    FATHER COYNE.
Get up please, son; let me finish giving her
Conditional absolution—

(STANTON *tightens his embrace on* KATHLEEN *again and
    glares at the priest like a cornered animal.*)

STANTON.
                    Absolve *her*, Father!

Absolve your God, why don't you, He did this!
When she found out the marriage was no good,
She packed her trunks upstairs. She meant to leave me.
She never died in drink! She never fell!
I flung her down the stairs to keep her here.
I thought she'd sprain her ankle— Don't come near me.
I'll spit in your face if you come near me, Father—

FATHER COYNE.

Go easy, son. Go easy.

HAGGERTY.

Get up now, Matt.

FATHER COYNE.

Yes, Matt. You have to follow Boylan to the precinct.
When there's a question of murder, it's the law.

(STANTON *relinquishes* KATHLEEN *to* FATHER COYNE,
and rises. STANTON *turns his back on his dead wife
and the priest as if in mortal offense.*)

STANTON.

Maria, lay my wife out on the bed
With some degree of decency, and spill
That bottle of the Worth perfume she loved
Over that bedspread that she was so proud of,
And sit with her until the coroner comes . . .
I will not have her stink, or lie alone—
        (*With great difficulty,* STANTON *brings himself to
        turn and look at his wife and the priest.*)
With all her sins on my head, and the world a desert.
        (STANTON *throws his arms out in a begging embrace
        and falls on his knees. Enter* MURPHY *and* QUINN,
        unnoticed by STANTON.)
Maisie, Jack. And Petey. Bessie, Father,
Help me, for the love of Jesus, help me.
Dear God in Heaven, help me and forgive me.

(*The* HAGGERTYS *rush to him and grasp his hands.* HAG-
        GERTY *raises him, and relinquishes him to* FATHER
        COYNE.)

MURPHY.
God have mercy on her. Our election's lost.

(STANTON *wheels around. His eyes meet with* QUINN'S.)

QUINN.
I never meant to do this to you, Matt.
I didn't know. I never meant to do it.
I only meant to look out for my good.
I'm nobody. I'm no one, if I'm not the mayor.
I'm nothing, Matt. I'm nobody. I'm nothing—

(STANTON *rakes* QUINN'S *face with a blind man's stare.
Exit* STANTON.)

FATHER COYNE.
Why are you standing round like imbeciles!
Carry her up the stairs, and lay her out
As Mattie asked you to.
    (HAGGERTY *and* BOYLE *lift* KATHLEEN, *and start up
the stairs with her.* MARIA *follows, her mouth in the
crook of her elbow, shaking with tears.* QUINN *and*
MURPHY, BESSIE *and* FATHER COYNE *look on from
below.*)
                 Well you may cry!
Cry for us all while you're at it. Cry for us all!

CURTAIN

HOGAN'S GOAT

ORIGINAL CAST

Première, November 11, 1965, American Place Theatre

Directed by Frederick Rolf

Scenery, lighting, and costumes by Kert Lundell

(*In order of appearance*)

MATTHEW STANTON, *leader of the Sixth Ward of Brooklyn*—Ralph Waite.

KATHLEEN STANTON, *his wife*—Fay Dunaway.

JOHN "BLACK JACK" HAGGERTY, *Assistant Ward Leader*—Roland Wood.

PETEY BOYLE, *a hanger-on of Stanton's*—Cliff Gorman.

BESSIE LEGG, *a back-room girl*—Michaele Myers.

MARIA HAGGERTY, *"Black Jack's" wife, the Stantons' janitor*—Grania O'Malley.

FATHER STANISLAUS COYNE, *Pastor of St. Mary Star of the Sea*—Barnard Hughes.

FATHER MALONEY, *Pastor of the All-night Printers' Church*—John Dorman.

EDWARD QUINN, *Mayor of Brooklyn*—Tom Ahearne.

JAMES "PALSY" MURPHY, *Boss of the city of Brooklyn*—Conrad Bain.

BILL, *a hanger-on of Quinn's*—Luke Wymbs.

ANN MULCAHY, *Father Coyne's housekeeper*—Agnes Young.

JOSEPHINE FINN, *Maria Haggerty's niece*—Tresa Hughes.

BOYLAN, *a policeman*—Tom Crane.

A DOCTOR—David Dawson.

CONSTITUENTS: Stan Sussman, *piano;* Eileen Fitzpatrick, Jack Fogarty, John Hoffmeister, Monica MacCormack, Michael Murray, Bruce Waite, Albert Shipley.

102

PRESET PROP LIST

Stage Right—Prop Table:
Champagne bottle (ASM fixes)
Quinn's ¼ filled cup of tea (cup, saucer, spoon)
Bible
Rosary
Bloody hanky
Typing paper
Tea tray (cream and sugar, 4 spoons, 4 cups on saucers)
Noisemakers on tray
Trunk key
Empty stein (for Petey)
1/3 filled whiskey (for Petey)
⅛ filled whiskey (for dance)
¼ filled brandy (for Kathleen)
1 cigarette and 7 matches (for Kathleen)
3 pillows (on 2nd shelf)
   Check On:
      Lantern (on flat)
      Wreath (on flat)
      Stool and prayer book (*off* R.)

Stage Left—Prop Table:
1 cigarette and matches (Kathleen)
4 cigars and cigarettes in box
Quinn's money
Empty stein
½ sandwich and ¾ hotdog roll on plate
Tray with:
   2 ½ filled beers
   ½ filled whiskey
   2 filled whiskies
   1 ½ filled whiskey
   1 ½ filled milk
Bessie's purse with key inside
Treasure box with:
   Marriage license (under secret bottom)
   Letter with tie
   2 rosaries

Dried camellia
Shamrock tie
Scorched letter
2 shot glasses (full)
Bessie's money (1 bill and 2 coins)
Blanket (2nd shelf)
Picnic basket (2nd shelf)
Ship lantern (on flat)

STANTON APARTMENT:
2 champagne glasses (on shelf)

On Table:
  Mirror
  Ashtray
  Cigarette box with 4 cigarettes
  Match box (striped cover)
Brandy glass (¼ full) on mantel
Small book open on window seat
Blue book on table ledge
Stack of clothes (off on small table)
Box of tissues (off on prop table)
Box of matches (off on prop table)
Blue towel (off on prop table)
Trunk (*off stage*)
Crucifix on mantel
4 black framed pictures on mantel
2 gold framed pictures on mantel
1 holy-water font on mantel

KITCHEN:
2 cups on saucers
2 spoons
Cream and sugar
Cake on plate (half sliced)
Brown teapot on mantel
Cannister of tea on mantel
Stove turned on

FOGARTY'S BACK ROOM:
Newspaper
Ashtray
Matches
Shot glass (full)

Check:
    2 towels
    Pitcher and bowl

SALOON :
4 ashtrays (3 small on side tables, 1 large on center table)
    Check:
        Top of piano, shamrocks
        Ivy above "Ladies' Entrance"

PROP MOVES

PRESET: *All props on and off stage, per page one*

ACT I

End of Act I—Scene 1 (Stanton Apartment)
  Nothing

End of Act I—Scene 2 (Saloon)
  Give "Set" to S.M. over s. l. headset, after getting from
    A.S.M.
  Take tray of dirty glasses down and wash

End of Act I—Scene 3 (Confessional)
  Nothing

During Act I—Scene 4 (Quinn-Murphy)
  Fill black kettle with hot water (wait until near very end of
    scene)

End of Act I—Scene 4
  Place black kettle on stove in kitchen; turn on stove
  Pick up chair in Fogarty's back room and carry off s. l.
  Take bowl and pitcher from Bill and place on lower s. r. prop-
    table
  Move tea tray from s. l. to s. r. prop table
  Rearrange noisemakers and glasses on s. r. prop table

End of Act I—Scene 5 (Wake)
  Help Josie Finn offstage in blackout

INTERMISSION

  Clear kitchen—2 cups, 2 saucers, 2 spoons, cake dish, sugar
    and creamer and torn hanky (found on floor), brown tea-
    pot, black kettle
  Replace tea cannister on mantel in kitchen
  Place 2 shot glasses and money on Quinn table (*off* s. l.)
  Clear Quinn table off s. l. of cup, saucer, spoon, ashtray,
    matches, newspaper and place all on s. r. prop table
  Place blue towel on Stanton apartment champagne glass ledge

Clear Stanton prop table of 2 champagne glasses, brandy glass, champagne bottle (place glasses on tray)

Pour beer in Petey's stein on S. R. prop table

Take tray containing 2 champagne glasses, 1 brandy glass, cake dish, 1 teacup from wake, 1 teacup and saucer from Quinn scene and brown teapot downstairs and wash

Pick up money on table and place under key

ACT II

End of Act II—Scene 1 (Quinn-Bessie)

Pick up stein and ashtray from small table S. R. in bar and then quietly lower table

Pick up 2 shot glasses from round center table

Leave stein and ashtray on S. L. prop table (2nd shelf)

Wash shot glasses

End of Act II—Scene 2 (Stanton Apartment)

Strike wreath from door of Haggertys' flat, hang on nail S. R.

During Act II—Scene 3 (After Jig)

Take tea tray from S. R. prop table and wipe off saucers and spoons

Leave saucers and spoons and sugar bowl on prop table

Take dirty cups and teapot and creamer downstairs and wash

After washing, bring back up together with round blue tray and place on 3rd shelf of S. R. prop table

After Bessie (Kathleen Scene)

Take Petey's stein down and wash and bring up—place on S. R. prop table, 2nd shelf

End of Act II—Scene 3 (Clambake)

1. Have key, flashlight and truck ready in Stanton apartment for blackout

2. Move chair to position horizontal and upstage of table

3. Place key on table under lamp

4. Pick up hat and purse from table and take off

5. Pick up shawl from window seat and take off

6. Pick up towel from ledge and take off

7. Place towel on Stanton prop table s. R.

8. Give set with flashlight to A.S.M. after Kathleen comes off and gets off her hat

9. Hand Kathleen first 4 clothes (orange, paisley, 2 black)

10. Hand Kathleen blue skirt

11. Hand Kathleen beige and flowered skirts with her red hat

12. Hand Kathleen velvet and beige shirt

13. Go down s. L. stairs, pick up glass and flower on s. L. prop table

14. Leave hanky and flashlight on s. R. prop table

15. Leave flower in Matt's dressing room

16. Leave hat, purse and shawl in Kathleen's dressing room

17. Wash glass

END OF SHOW

Strike whiskey glass from kitchen mantel
Pick up hat and gloves and purse from stairs
Clean out bar ashtrays
Unpack trunk—check picture frame and crucifix
Replace mirror and cigarette box on table
Clean out ashtray
Strike key, clothes from trunk and black shawl from trunk
Put key on s. R. prop table, 2nd shelf
Take black shawl, hat, gloves and purse to Kathleen
Repack treasure box, put s. L.
Wash whiskey glass

COSTUMES

KATHLEEN
- 1 gold dress-lace top
- 1 green skirt
- 1 beige blouse
- 1 purple velvet dress-hat
- 1 gold stole
- 1 black lace stole

BESSIE
- 1 purple skirt
- 1 purple blouse
- 1 feather boa
- 1 purple shawl
- 1 feathered hat

MARIA
- 1 black dress
- 1 white apron

ANN MULCAHY
- 1 black skirt
- 1 black shawl
- 1 blue blouse

JOSIE FINN
- 1 black skirt
- 1 black blouse
- 1 black shawl

BARMAID
- 1 maroon skirt
- 1 maroon blouse
- 1 apron

GIRL CONSTITUENT
- 1 gold skirt
- 1 black blouse

STANTON
- 1 3-piece brown suit
- 1 2-piece blue suit

1 striped vest
1 brocade vest
1 hat

HAGGERTY
1 gray jacket
1 gray pants
1 black vest

PETEY BOYLE
1 brown jacket
1 black pants
1 black vest
1 brown cap

FATHER COYNE
1 black cassock
1 black topcoat
1 biretta

FATHER MALONEY
1 black cassock
1 biretta

QUINN
1 morning coat
1 striped pants
1 brocade vest
1 top hat
1 cane

MURPHY
1 3-piece brown check suit
1 hat
White gloves

BILL
1 chauffeur's jacket
1 black pants
1 cap

BOYLAN
1 2-piece policeman's uniform
1 bobby's hat
night stick and belt

CONSTITUENTS
- 1 3-piece gray stripe suit
- 1 3-piece gray suit
- 1 3-piece brown suit
- 1 3-piece black tweed suit
- 1 rust jacket, pants, cap
- 1 brown cord jacket, pants, **vest**

EXTRA COSTUMES
- 1 brown dress
- 1 2-piece green woman's suit
- 1 green skirt
- 1 morning coat, pants, vest
- 1 cassock
- 1-3-piece brown-and-red stripe **suit**
- 1 black dress
- 1 green jacket

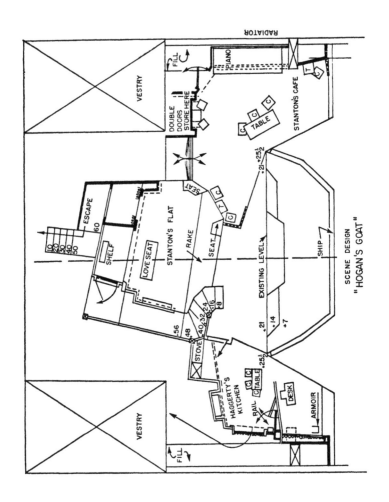

SCENE DESIGN
"HOGAN'S GOAT"

CPSIA information can be obtained
at www.ICGtesting.com
Printed in the USA
BVHW062156050522
636286BV00011B/194